WEDDING BELLS AT THE STABLES ON MUDDYPUDDLE LANE

Heart-warming, uplifting romance

Etti Summers

CHAPTER ONE

Julie Richards took a hankie out of her bag and wiped the tears from her cheeks. She really should stop being so self-indulgent, she thought. This constant crying wasn't doing anyone any good, least of all her. She knew that Isaac was starting to despair that she'd ever get over her grief.

To be honest, she was beginning to fear the same thing.

But there was no expiry date on mourning someone, was there? You didn't get to a certain point after losing a loved one and suddenly wake up the next day with the grief magically lifted. If she'd discovered one thing since she'd learnt of Emrys's death, it was that grief was a tricky thing to get a grip of. Some days she wasn't so bad and she'd think she'd turned the corner, but there were others where she didn't want to get out of bed.

Today was particularly difficult, because today was the first anniversary of his passing, and the only way she could feel close to him was to visit the one place that she and Emrys had returned to again and again – their special place.

Julie sank down onto the grass and stared across the valley. She was sitting some way above the same lonely layby where they used to come all those years ago. Sometimes they would sit in his car and kiss, other times they would take a walk up the hill and make out in the long grass, with the wind sighing around them as they whispered their love for each other.

It was the only place she felt vaguely close to him. She would have visited his grave if she could, but he'd been buried far away in New Zealand and she couldn't face travelling all that way on her own to say a final goodbye. So she'd come here instead, to a hillside not far from the quaint village of Picklewick, to mark the day that Emrys had died.

Out of necessity, they'd had to meet out of town, away from prying eyes, because she and Emrys hadn't been able to have a normal relationship – her marriage to Stephen had made sure of that. Even now, all these years later, she felt incredibly disgusted and ashamed of her behaviour. But she'd been pulled towards Emrys as strongly and as irrevocably as a star was sucked into a black hole, and there hadn't been a damned thing she had been able to do about it. Despite having been married to Stephen (patient, kind, loving Stephen) for three years, she had fallen desperately in love with Emrys.

He had been her deepest love, although not her only love, because after she'd finally found the strength to drive him away, she had tried so very hard to be the wife that Stephen deserved.

It wasn't as though she didn't love her husband. She did – she would never have married him if she hadn't. But she had also never experienced a passion like she had for Emrys. He had consumed her, heart, body and soul, like a wildfire raging through her life, out of control, burning hot and savage, and she had been helpless in the face of those ravenous flames.

Then she had discovered she was pregnant, and everything changed.

From out of depths that she hadn't known she'd possessed, she'd found the strength to tell Emrys she didn't love him – at least, not enough to emigrate to New Zealand with him. He'd begged and pleaded, scalding her with his hot, raw pain, but she hadn't relented. It was the only thing in the whole affair that she didn't hate herself for, because how could she have left Stephen when she had his baby growing inside her? She might have been prepared to deprive him of his wife, but she couldn't, in all conscience, deprive him of his son.

She'd lied through her teeth to push Emrys away, and she had stayed in the

UK and stayed in her marriage, and vowed to be the best wife that she could possibly be to make up for her failings. She had buried her love for Emrys as deeply as she could, and had concentrated on her marriage and all that was good about it. She'd been happy and so had Stephen, and she'd kept her vow for all this time – until she'd learned that Emrys was dead and her world had fallen apart.

Until that point, the thought of Emrys dying hadn't entered her mind. Whenever she thought of him (which hadn't been as often as she used to as the years sped by), he was still the handsome, witty, passionate man she had fallen in love with. In her mind he'd not aged, although she imagined that he would have moved on – wife, family, new career – but the details of his new life in a far-off country were hazy.

Never once had she been tempted to look him up or track him down. In the early days the internet had been non-existent so the option wouldn't have been available to her anyway, and as time went on and social media exploded, she'd still not gone looking for him for fear of what she might find. She didn't want to see photos of him with a wife, or with his children, or looking old. She wanted the image of him that she held in her mind to stay pristine and unsullied by the passage of time.

So it was a terrible shock when his daughter had contacted her at the end of last year. Julie could have kicked herself for making it so easy to be found. But then again, maybe a part of her hadn't wanted to move out of the house she'd been living in since she and Stephen had got married or change the phone number they'd always had, just in case Emrys had wanted to…

That was a silly notion. She'd broken Emrys's heart when she'd told him that it was Stephen she truly loved, and he'd left for the other side of the world believing he'd been nothing more to her than a brief affair. Why would he ever have wanted to get in touch with her again?

He never did – but his daughter had, delivering the awful and incomprehensible news that Emrys had passed away. She'd found Julie's details hidden amongst some of his personal papers, with the instruction that Julie should be informed when he died. But his daughter hadn't found it until a few months after his death, and Julie couldn't help feeling desolate that she'd gone about her normal everyday life for all those weeks without the slightest hint that Emrys was no longer in this world. Surely she should have known? Surely some sixth sense should have told her that the man she'd loved so comprehensively had left this mortal coil?

It had been her lack of awareness, plus the message that Emrys had wanted her to know that he'd never stopped loving her, that had been her undoing. As grief had sunk its claws deeper into her heart, her life and the lives of her husband and son had unravelled. Stephen had left her, and Isaac had moved halfway across the country to be closer to her, giving up his home and his business because he was so concerned about her.

Julie dabbed her eyes again, marvelling how she still had so many tears left. She'd thought she'd done all her crying for Emrys when she had told him it was over. In the days, weeks, and months afterwards, she'd wept in secret. Whenever Stephen asked her what was wrong, she had blamed it on the pregnancy hormones making her weepy.

Since Emrys's daughter had phoned, Julie felt as though it was only yesterday that she'd pushed him away, that the intervening years had been a dream. And grief had risen up and swamped her. It was only a slim consolation that Emrys's daughter had reassured her he'd had a good life and had been happy, and he'd gone on to love again and had been loved in return.

Julie had been happy herself; she would be lying if she said she hadn't. Over the years her love for her husband had deepened, and eventually it had come to rival and even exceed the love she'd felt for Emrys. Stephen had been happy too, and it was this knowledge which convinced her that she had done the right thing in not choosing Emrys. Stephen loved being a father and had been a caring and involved dad. Whenever she saw him and Isaac together, she knew she couldn't have taken that away from him.

It was a pity everything had fallen apart now, when things were so good between them. Stephen had planned to retire when he reached sixty and they were going to take the opportunity (before grandchildren came along) to travel.

They'd been so looking forward to spending their twilight years together.

Now, it seemed, they were going to spend them apart.

Desperately sad, Julie got up from the patch of grass she'd been sitting on, feeling lonelier than she'd ever felt in her life. She missed Emrys, goddamit.

But what was worse was that she missed Stephen **more**.

'What do you think?' Petra asked, moving a vase of flowers that was sitting on the dining table a few centimetres to the left, and standing back to eye it critically.

'It looks fabulous,' Nelly said, and Isaac nodded.

'It does look good,' he agreed. 'Just make sure you turn all the lights on when you take your photos – no matter how bright it is outside, you'll need some help to ensure the images do the place justice.'

'Have you found much that needs doing?' Petra wanted to know. Now that the work had been more or less completed on the barn conversion, she, Nelly and Isaac were checking the three cottages to make sure there weren't any issues which needed addressing. Nelly called it snagging – Petra called it doing the job properly. Luckily, the stables on Muddypuddle Lane had an excellent architect in Isaac, and Nelly and her firm of builders had proved to be thorough, efficient and extremely competent.

'Not a great deal,' Nelly said. 'I'll email the list over to you, and I'll copy you in, Isaac, for your records.'

'Like what?' he asked.

'A tap in the downstairs cloakroom of cottage number three isn't quite square on, and the door in one of the bedrooms in the second cottage will catch once the rug is down if a bit isn't shaved off the bottom. I can't see anything that needs attention in this one, though.'

They were standing in the living-cum-dining room of the first cottage, the one that Petra was scrambling to furnish in order to take photos to upload to the various holiday rental websites. She didn't intend to officially open until after her wedding in three weeks' time, but she wanted to get as much done as she possibly could beforehand. Then she could turn her attention to her nuptials, because she hadn't even bought a dress yet. She had suggested to Amos that she wore what she was happiest in – jodhpurs and Wellington boots – but her uncle had thrown a fit, and her groom hadn't been too enamoured with the idea either.

'I want to see you in a wedding dress,' Harry had said, taking her in his arms and kissing her. 'I don't care if you think I'm old-fashioned.'

'White doesn't suit me,' she'd retorted, only to be informed that he didn't care what colour it was, as long as it was a dress fit for the occasion of celebrating their marriage. Although he did have one caveat – he didn't want her to wear black.

Even Petra wouldn't have dreamt of wearing black to her own wedding! She didn't want people to think they were attending a funeral.

Nelly popped her iPad in the bag. 'I think that's it for today,' she said. 'I'll send a couple of guys around tomorrow to finish the snagging, then you're good to go.'

Petra wasn't so sure. She knew what she was doing when it came to horses and running the stables, but operating holiday rentals wasn't her area of expertise and she was worried she'd missed something or that she wasn't pitching it right.

Take the welcome basket she'd planned on providing, for instance...Was it okay to pop a bottle of wine in? How about the complementary chocolates? Was she overdoing it? Or not doing enough?

'You wouldn't like to test run this cottage for me, would you?' she asked, as an idea occurred to her. 'I could do with someone staying for a night or two to give me an honest opinion. I'd hate for our first guests to give us a bad review because we didn't provide a salad spinner, or something.'

'A salad spinner?' Isaac looked baffled.

'Amos was wittering on about one the other day. It shakes off all the water from your salad leaves after you've washed them.' Petra pulled a face. She honestly didn't give a hoot about salad spinners, but then again she wasn't the one who did the cooking, so perhaps she was being unfair.

'Is that really a thing?' Nelly asked.

'Apparently so.'

'Gosh. What happened to dabbing them dry with a clean tea towel?'

Petra shrugged. 'My thoughts exactly! So, what do you say about a trial run?'

'I think it's a marvellous idea to take a cottage for a spin, but we're probably not the best ones to do it,' Nelly said. 'We're too close to the project, don't you think so, Isaac?'

'Definitely! You need fresh eyes, and preferably from someone with no preconceptions,' Isaac advised.

'That's not going to be easy – everyone I could possibly ask has been involved with the conversion in one way or another.' Petra thought back to the barn clearing that had taken place earlier in the year. Loads of people had turned up to help them empty the old cow shed and get it ready for Nelly's builders to move in and do their bit.

Petra had been pregnant at the time and had been sternly warned by both Harry and Amos not to do too much. Gosh, she couldn't believe that little Amory was already nearly three months old. And neither could she believe that Nelly and her crew had managed to complete the job in such a short amount of time. Nelly had warned her that it might take as long as six months to convert a cow shed into three holiday cottages, but she'd pulled out all the stops and it had taken fourteen weeks from start to finish.

Petra gazed around in awe. She still found it hard to believe that the gorgeous living room she was currently standing in, with the stunning view across the valley, had once housed cattle. The transformation was unbelievable.

She was particularly pleased with **this** cottage because it was furnished. It had been a bit of a rush to get it done, with Petra having to do a great deal of something she wasn't terribly keen on – shopping. She loved buying horsey stuff and the last time she'd gone to The Horse of the Year Show she'd spent a fortune, but shopping for furniture and cushions? Meh, not so much.

Still, she'd done it, and now that everything was in place all she needed to do was to duplicate it for the other two cottages. October, who was her Girl Friday around the stables, was trying to persuade her to furnish each one in a different style, even if it was something as simple as changing the colour scheme, but Petra wasn't sure she could be bothered, although she had to admit that it would look better on the website to have each cottage with a different theme.

'I've got an idea,' Isaac said. 'How would you feel about my mum and dad staying for a weekend? I'm sure they'll give you their honest opinion, even if it was their son who designed the build.'

Petra noticed that Nelly was giving him an odd look.

'Er, won't that be a bit difficult?' Nelly said. 'They're not...um...together, in case you've forgotten.'

Isaac was grinning from ear to ear. 'That's the point. Are you game for a spot of matchmaking?' he asked Petra.

Petra grinned at him. He already knew she was. Before she'd met Harry love and romance hadn't been on her radar; now however, she couldn't get enough of it.

'Am I ever,' she declared rubbing her hands together. She was looking forward to this. She wasn't aware of the details, but she knew that Isaac's parents had split up a while ago. If Isaac wanted help in getting them back together, she was in.

She was just about to ask him what he was planning, when she heard a baby's cross wail. 'Oh dear, I think someone might be ready for a feed,' she said, as Amos appeared holding a grizzling infant in his arms.

Petra reached for her son, and he immediately began to cry louder. 'He's hungry, aren't you, baby?'

'I think that's our cue to leave,' Nelly said. 'Anyway, I quite fancy some lunch myself.' Turning to Isaac, she said, 'Do you have to rush off?'

'Definitely not. Lunch sounds good. Bye Petra, bye Amos, and I'm not going to leave you out, little man,' Isaac said to Amory, chucking the baby under the chin.

Amory blarted his indignation and Petra laughed. 'Come on, poppet, let's get you fed, shall we?' She headed outside to the bench next to the living room window and sat down.

Amos joined her.

'They make a lovely couple, don't they?' she said to her uncle as she undid her shirt and shifted the baby into position. Very soon, contented slurps filled the air.

'They do,' Amos agreed, watching Nelly and Isaac walk along the path, heading for their respective vehicles. 'How did the snagging go?'

It was amazing how quickly both she, Harry and Amos had picked up building jargon, Petra mused. Six months ago, she wouldn't have had a clue what that meant.

'There's not much, and nothing to be done in the first cottage, so after I've fed Mr Greedy here, I can go ahead and take the photos for the website.'

'Luca's getting on okay with it, is he?'

'I think so. It was looking really professional last time I saw it. It's so kind of him to help – I wouldn't know where to begin.'

'What does he do for a living exactly?' Amos asked.

'No idea.' Petra shifted the baby to the other breast and when he was settled, she said, 'Whatever it is, he's successful at it.' Luca had begun stabling his horse, Midnight, with them shortly before Petra had taken October on, and she'd got to know him fairly well over the course of this year, and especially since he and October had become an item.

'Do you think they'll get married?' Amos asked.

'October and Lucas? Possibly. You've got weddings on the brain,' Petra teased.

'Someone has to, because if it was left to you, you'd nip into the church on Sunday while still wearing your riding gear and expect the vicar to fit the ceremony in between the sermon and lunch.'

Petra stuck her tongue out at him.

'Be careful the wind doesn't change and your face will be stuck like that,' he warned. 'Right, when you've finished feeding the baby, you need to have something to eat yourself before you start taking photos. I've made some chicken and vegetable soup, and we've got some freshly baked rolls to go with it.'

Petra gently bumped his shoulder with hers. 'What would I do without you?' she said fondly, as he got to his feet.

'I'll go up to the house and begin warming it,' he said. 'Don't be long.'

'We won't.'

Petra waited for him to leave, then she leaned her head against the wall, closed her eyes and breathed deeply, enjoying the peace. A light breeze blew gently across her face, lifting the hairs that had escaped from her ponytail so they tickled her cheek, and she brushed them away. Aside from her son's contented suckling, the only other noises were the distant bleating of sheep on the hillside above and the chirping of birds in the hedgerow.

Feeling so happy she could burst, Petra thought how incredibly lucky she was. She was about to marry the love of her life, she had the most gorgeous baby in the world, and an uncle who was like a father; the stables was doing well and she had a brand new venture to look forward to.

For Petra, life was wonderful, and she was truly blessed.

'Dad, I've been thinking,' Isaac said as soon as Stephen answered the phone, and Stephen winced. In his experience, when someone says that they've been thinking, the person who said it usually had some hare-brained idea in mind.

'What about?' he asked cautiously, hoping it didn't involve him. He loved his son to the moon and back, but he didn't want to be roped into anything. He was quite happy as he was.

Actually, that was a lie – Stephen wasn't happy at all, and he hadn't been since Julie had announced that she'd been unfaithful and that her lover was dead. Admittedly, the affair had taken place before Isaac was born, but considering Stephen had only found out about it relatively recently, to him it felt as though it had just happened.

When he'd demanded times, dates, places (he'd wanted to know every sordid detail), and she'd informed him that she'd only ended it because she'd been pregnant, it had briefly entered his head that he wasn't Isaac's father and that this Emrys fella was. But Julie had quickly disavowed him of the notion, in a not particularly nice way. She'd informed him that if Isaac **had** been Emrys's child she would have gone to New Zealand with Emrys, because the only thing which had prevented her from leaving was that she hadn't wanted to deprive Stephen of his son.

Words had failed him.

He'd been so hurt it had taken his breath away. Even after nine months, the pain hadn't lessened. In fact, he believed it had grown worse. With every passing day he missed Julie more and more, and some days he wondered how he could go on without her.

In the beginning, his hurt had been overlain with bitterness and betrayal, and anger, too. But as the weeks had turned into months the anger had faded, as had the bitterness, until all he'd been left with was a deep and abiding sorrow and a persistent ache in his heart.

God, how he missed her. He missed talking to her about his day, snuggling up to her at night, her ready smile, her calm and gentle manner.

Stephen had come to realise that he was grieving for her as though she were dead, and in a way maybe that was true, because the woman he'd known and loved for all these years hadn't been the woman he'd thought she was. He was grieving for her, and for the life they'd had together. He was also mourning the loss of their future, which he was now having to face alone.

'Dad, did you hear what I said?'

'Huh? Sorry Isaac, you cut out for a moment,' Stephen lied. 'Run that past me again?'

'I was saying that Petra at the stables on Muddypuddle Lane wants someone who isn't connected with the barn conversion to stay in one of the cottages for a couple of nights to road test it, so to speak. You know, make sure everything works, that she hasn't forgotten anything...You get the drift.'

'I do indeed.'

'I've got to warn you, one of the selling points of the cottage is that it's a complete getaway from it all – there's no wifi and the phone signal can be a bit hit and miss. There is a TV though, and Petra has stocked the place with books and board games, so hopefully you'll manage to keep yourself amused for the duration. What do you say?'

'I suppose I could.'

'Don't sound so enthusiastic,' Isaac said. 'You could do with a break, and it's not as though it's going to cost you anything. Plus, you'll be doing me a favour: I trust your opinion and I know you'll be honest and fair.'

Despite his initial impulse to refuse because he didn't fancy going on holiday by himself, Stephen felt flattered that his son valued his opinion. Maybe if he looked on it as a job and not a weekend break, he'd be more inclined to go.

He tried the idea out for size and decided he could cope. He'd be methodical about it and check that everything worked, even if it was something he wouldn't normally use, such as a trouser press – did they still have those? He'd even try out the microwave if there was one, although that was another thing he wouldn't normally use on holiday; on those occasions where he and Julie had rented an apartment or a cottage, neither of them had wanted to do much in the way of cooking, preferring to eat out.

Stephen sighed and pushed thoughts of Julie and past holidays to the back of his mind. He had to look forward, not back;

dwelling on the past never did anyone any good.

'Did you say it was in Picklewick?' he asked.

'A couple of miles outside.'

'That's right, I remember now. You've done a few more jobs since then.'

Isaac chuckled. 'I have, thank goodness. But I was back there this morning with Nelly, to do some snagging.'

'How is Nelly?' Stephen asked.

Isaac had fallen in love with Nelly at university when she was on the same course as him, but her father's illness had forced her to drop out and she'd subsequently taken over her dad's construction business and they'd lost touch. Isaac had bumped into her again when he'd drawn up the architectural plans for the barn conversion and Nelly's firm had been employed as the builder. Their love had reignited, and they'd been inseparable ever since. Stephen had a lot of time for Nelly – she was a lovely girl and he could tell she was head-over-heels in love with his son.

'She's good,' Isaac said. 'We're going out for a meal tonight.'

'Somewhere nice?'

'The Black Horse in Picklewick. You should have a meal there when you stay at the cottage. The food is pretty good and so is the atmosphere.'

'I might just do that,' Stephen said, warming to the idea.

Picklewick was only nine miles away, but he remembered Isaac telling him that the stables were halfway up the side of a hill, surrounded by farmland and with moorland above, so it would feel like he was in the middle of nowhere.

'Okay, you're on – I'll give the cottage a go if you think it'll help your clients. And who can say no to a freebie?' he added.

'Petra was hoping you could do this weekend,' his son said, sounding so delighted that it made him wonder if Isaac had been worried about him.

Stephen had to admit that he hadn't exactly been the life and soul of the party lately, so this break might do him good. Since last November he'd been stuck in a rut, not wanting to do anything apart from go to work. Even during the six weeks of the school summer holidays, which was finally coming to an end, he'd not felt like going away. The furthest he'd gone had been to the DIY store on the outskirts of town, and he'd only done that because he wanted a bookshelf to store all his school stuff on.

He had even gone into work once or twice, so that showed how the time had dragged. Oh, well, at least his classroom looked good and the displays on the wall were top-notch, ready for the start of the new term in September. He'd also caught up on all the paperwork, which was usually a slog he tried to avoid until the last minute, and he had to rush to complete it.

When he'd stayed so long at school the other day that the caretaker had kicked him out, Stephen had been forced to admit that he was lonely. Maybe he should get back out there into the world of meeting people and dating, but he didn't have the energy or the inclination.

In some ways, he regretted his knee-jerk reaction in leaving Julie, but he'd felt so hurt and betrayed, and he still did.

Silently, he shook his head. What was done, was done, and there was no going back. In fact, it might be time to consider getting a divorce. End it once and for all. There was no point in hanging onto a marriage that was dead in the water, so they may as well formalise the end of their union. After all, he could foresee him and Julie only having to spend time together in the future, if Isaac and Nelly got married or gave them grandchildren.

Seeing his son so happy made Stephen's heart ache. He vividly remembered what he and Julie had been like in the early days, how in love they'd been. How they hadn't been able to keep their hands off each other.

Things had calmed down somewhat once they'd got married, but that was only to be expected. The first flush of passion had mellowed into a different kind of love as they had learned to live together. They'd had their ups and downs, of course – every married couple did – but they'd worked through them and had come out the other side.

They had been happy, hadn't they? He hadn't imagined it. Julie couldn't have been that good an actress; she'd told him time and time again that she loved him and he'd believed her – he'd had no reason not to. Until recently. And even now, he found it hard to believe that she hadn't meant it. They had been together for nearly forty years, and he could have sworn those years had been happy ones.

Or, so he had believed.

He snorted bitterly. It was all a lie. It had to have been, otherwise Julie wouldn't have fallen into the arms of another man.

Suddenly Stephen felt weary and worn down, and the thought of living the rest of his life on his own sent a wave of depression through him. He had nothing to get up for in the morning – apart from his job – and it was incredibly sad to think that the only reason he was looking forward to the start of the new term was because it meant he wouldn't be alone all day. What kind of a life was that?

Even the brief spark of interest that the mention of a couple of days away had caused, didn't last. He wasn't sure that spending a long weekend in the middle of nowhere on his own would do much to help his mood, but he'd agreed to it now. Going back on his word for no real reason might ring an alarm bell in Isaac's head and the last thing Stephen wanted was for his son to worry about him.

He would just have to make the best of it. With scant enthusiasm he went to the cupboard under the stairs to root out his hiking boots. At least he could get a bit of exercise in the fresh air, and he guessed anything was better than sitting at home staring at the four walls.

CHAPTER TWO

'Tea, coffee, sugar, wine, chocolates, a loaf of bread, cake...' Petra was standing in the kitchen of one of the recently converted cottages, staring critically at the welcome pack. 'And there's milk in the fridge, both cow and soya, and butter. Have we forgotten anything?' She patted the little bundle of cosily-wrapped baby who was snuggled against her chest in his sling, and swayed gently from side to side. If only he'd stay asleep for another half an hour.

'I think it's more than generous,' Amos said. 'Home-made cake and freshly baked bread... hmph!'

Her uncle was grizzling because he was the one who'd whisked up the cake and had baked the loaf, but she could tell he didn't mean it. He was as keen to get this right as she was, and there was only one opportunity to make a good impression, as he kept telling her. Besides, he loved a spot of baking, did Amos, and he was good at it. Petra was certain that their guests would appreciate the homely touch.

Fresh flowers picked from the garden behind the farmhouse, with greenery gathered from the hedgerows while she was out on her early morning ride, made the living room look welcoming and cheerful, and she'd also remembered to leave a small booklet on the sideboard with information about things to do and local attractions. As an added bonus, she was offering a half price ride too, so that might appeal to some people.

'Eggs!' she cried, suddenly remembering. The stables had a resident flock of chickens looked after by a noisy cockerel called Fred. As the hens laid on a regular basis there were always eggs to spare, and she'd planned to include half a dozen in the welcome basket. If the guests wanted any more, they could always buy them from her.

'I've boxed them up ready,' Amos said. 'They're in the kitchen up at the house. I'll fetch them in a minute, and I've also swapped half a dozen for some of Walter York's pears. I thought we'd have poached pears after dinner this evening.'

'How is Walter?' Petra asked. Although he lived in Lilac Tree Farm further along

Muddypuddle Lane, she hardly ever saw the old man himself. Just his sheep.

'Not good,' Amos said. 'He's struggling a bit. I get the impression he's not well.'

'Is there anything we can do to help?'

Amos shook his head. 'I did offer, but you know how stubborn and independent he can be.'

Petra had heard, but she didn't know Walter particularly well. In all the years she'd lived at the stables, she'd only spoken to him a dozen or so times. He tended to keep himself to himself. She knew he'd lost his wife years ago, and that he had a grown-up son who was a chef in London, but that was about it. The poor chap didn't have much in the way of family, and she'd also heard that a long-lost brother of his had died last year, so she felt rather sorry for him. But Walter was a stubborn old fellow from what Amos had told her and didn't; take kindly to offers of help. Often, the only reason she knew he was still around was because his sheep would be moved from one field to another. Occasionally she'd hear his Land Rover in the lane, and once or twice she'd catch a glimpse of him which, considering they were neighbours, wasn't much.

'We really should plant a pear tree of our own,' Amos said. 'How about if we plant one down here?' He pointed to the far end of the sloping lawn.

'We could, I suppose,' Petra said.

She didn't usually take much notice of the gardening side of things, leaving that to Amos, who had a thriving veggie patch outside the back door. But she had taken an interest in the landscaping around the newly converted cottages, wanting everything to be just right. It was early days yet, as the area around the former cow shed was still rather bare, although Amos, with the help of October's mum Lena, had turned a tump of rubble that had been excavated from the floor of the barn into a rockery, and it now sported a variety of small alpine plants which were gradually establishing themselves. By next spring it should look wonderful.

None of the cottages had much of a garden, but they all had their own private seating areas out the back, which consisted of a patio surrounded by flowering shrubs, and there was a lawned area to the front where the planting had been kept deliberately low-key so as to take advantage of the wonderful views across the valley.

'Next month I'll pop some spring bulbs in,' Amos said, gazing out of the window. 'And Lena said she's going to separate some of her perennials, so I can have those as well. It should look lovely.'

Petra moved closer to her uncle and slipped an arm through his. 'It looks lovely already,' she said. 'You've done a wonderful job.'

'**We**,' he amended. '**We've** done a wonderful job. It's taken all of us to get this project up and running – you, Harry, me, Nathan, October, Luca, Timothy, Charity, Lena...'

Petra knew he was right. They'd come a long way from Harry's vague idea of turning an unused and semi-derelict outbuilding into holiday homes, and everyone had helped to make the dream become a reality.

They stood in companiable silence for a few more minutes, then Amos checked his watch.

'When are Isaac's parents arriving?' he asked. 'If there's anything left to do, we'd better get a move on.'

'Ah, this is where things might be a bit tricky,' Petra said with a grimace. 'They're not arriving at the same time. Isaac's mum will be arriving first – Isaac is bringing her because she hasn't got a car – then his dad should hopefully turn up.'

Amos stepped back and shot her a look. 'Why do I get the feeling there's something going on?'

Petra smiled sheepishly. 'Because there is?'

Her uncle inhaled deeply then let the breath out in a sigh. 'You'd better tell me.'

'Isaac's mum and dad aren't exactly together,' she began.

'In what way?'

'They are separated and have been for about nine months.'

'They must still get along,' Amos pointed out, 'for them to be having a weekend break together.'

'Er, not exactly. The split wasn't amicable.'

'Then why would they—? Oh, **I see**, this is a reconciliation? I hope it works out for them.'

Petra shook her head. 'It's not a reconciliation. They don't know the other is going to be here. You see, Isaac thinks they still love each other, but things have gone too far for either of them to make the first move – so he's doing it for them.'

'Is that wise?'

'Maybe not, but considering they're not speaking anyway, I doubt if it'll make things any worse.'

'Don't be too sure,' Amos warned. 'Meddling in other people's relationships is never a good idea.'

'I'm not meddling – Isaac is.'

'You're helping him.'

'I'll deny all knowledge,' Petra said. 'As far as I'm concerned, Isaac suggested

that his parents give one of the cottages
a trial run, and that's the end of my
involvement.'

'I bet it won't be,' Amos said. 'You've
become a right little matchmaker
recently. Mark my words, not everyone
appreciates it. I certainly wouldn't.'

'It's lucky that there isn't anyone for me
to matchmake you with then, isn't it?' she
replied with a smirk.

But when a faint hint of colour spread
across Amos's whiskery face, Petra began
to wonder...

Dear god! Julie was seriously tempted to
demand that Isaac turned the car around
and take her straight back home, but the
only thing preventing her was that she'd

have to explain the reason why. And she didn't fancy telling her son that the road they were driving along was the very road where she and Emrys used to meet. Only the other day she'd walked up the same road, having caught the bus to Picklewick, and had climbed over the stile near the layby and scrambled up the hill to sit in the long grass and have a good weep.

She should have put two and two together and realised that the barn conversion that Isaac had drawn up the plans for was just down the road from **their** favourite meeting place.

The irony and the coincidence might have made her smile, if it wasn't for the fact that she felt like bawling.

How on earth was she supposed to spend three nights here?

She'd lose her mind.

But she didn't have a great deal of choice, did she?

However, as Isaac turned the car off the road and onto Muddypuddle Lane to drive up a rutted track, she began to have second thoughts. Maybe it wouldn't be so bad, after all; the layby was some distance up ahead and it wasn't as though she'd be going that way, because if she wanted a meal out or to mooch around some shops, Picklewick village was in the other direction.

'Is that the cottage?' she asked, seeing an old stone building just off the road. It didn't look all that big from this angle, and it appeared to be rather ramshackle, but...

'No, the stables are up there. See?' Isaac pointed to a group of buildings halfway up the side of the hill. 'The cottages are to the right, but you can't really see them from here.'

Even better, Julie thought. If they were hidden from the road, then the road would be hidden from them, and hopefully her memories would be too.

Shortly they were pulling off the lane and trundling down a narrow, tarmacked track which bypassed the stables and ended in a small parking area just big enough for three vehicles. Ahead, she could see a path leading to a row of cottages through a gap in a hedge.

Even from this distance they looked lovely, and Julie was surprised to find that she couldn't wait to see inside. She hadn't shown this much interest in anything for a long time.

Isaac lifted her case and a box containing foodstuff out of the boot and slammed it shut. 'Crumbs! What have you got in here?' he cried, hefting the box. 'It weighs a ton.'

'Gin.' She'd packed some food for appearance's sake, but she suspected she wouldn't bother to eat a great deal of it – she hadn't had much of an appetite since Stephen had walked out.

'Do you think you're going to need it?' Isaac joked, setting the case down on its wheels and lengthening the handle.

'Probably.' She gazed around, her eyes scanning the valley. 'It's so peaceful,' she said, changing the subject as the silence washed over her.

On second thoughts, maybe it would be **too** quiet she mused apprehensively, as she realised there wouldn't be anyone in the other cottages yet and she'd be here on her own. She wasn't used to such isolation and the thought worried her. If Stephen had been with her, she wouldn't have given a hoot about being so far from civilisation, but he wasn't, so it was a genuine concern.

'Er, I think I might be a bit lonely,' she said. 'It's incredibly quiet. And I'm not too happy about not being able to use my phone.'

'I didn't say you **couldn't** use it, Mum,' Isaac said, giving her that sideways look of his that made her feel like a little old lady – which she most definitely was not! 'All I said was, that the reception around here could be a bit dodgy. You might have to wave your phone out of the bedroom window or walk up to the house to get a decent signal, for instance.'

'That's no good if there's a prowler outside, is it?' Against her better judgement, Julie allowed her son to lead her along the path towards the cottages.

He gave her another sideways look, this time accompanied by a sigh. 'There's hardly likely to be a prowler, although you might find a goat wandering about. She's not supposed to, but she's a right little escape artist.'

'A goat,' Julie repeated flatly. She didn't know how she felt about goats. The closest she'd ever come to one was when she'd eaten a goat's cheese salad. And she suspected that the lamb dish she'd once had in a restaurant in Cyprus might have actually been goat.

'Princess is harmless enough,' Isaac told her.

'Back to my prowler problem,' Julie continued, as they came to a halt outside the front door.

'You haven't got a prowler problem.' He glanced at his watch, and she guessed he was eager to get her settled in so he could be off.

The door to the cottage was unlocked and he shouldered his way inside.

Julie frowned and followed him. 'Is the door always kept unlocked?'

'No, Mum, it isn't. Petra said she'd leave it open, and could we come up to the house to collect the keys? I told you she's not long had a baby, didn't I? She's up to her eyes at the moment trying to get everything ready, so before you start thinking that the cottages won't be secure, don't worry – she's got a system in place for when paying guests arrive.'

Julie was relieved, because that was the first thing she would have mentioned in her report.

'I'll leave your case here, and we can go on up to the house,' Isaac said.

'Do you mind if I have a quick look round first?' Julie asked. She had to admit that it all looked very nice.

The front door opened up into a small hallway with the stairs leading off and a cloak room to the side, and another door led into a bright and airy living room with a picture window to the front. There was a small television, and two squashy sofas, a bookcase laden with both fiction and non-fiction, and a shelf underneath holding an assortment of board games. The other end of the room held a dining table and four chairs, with French doors opening out onto a compact paved area with further seating and a hammock. The hammock was a sweet touch, but she knew she wouldn't try it.

To the left of the dining area was a small but well-equipped and perfectly modern kitchen, and its window also looked out into the little private garden.

'There are two bedrooms upstairs, both with their own bathrooms,' Isaac informed her as he propped her case at the bottom of the stairs, and she heard the pride in his voice.

'It's lovely,' she said. 'You've done a good job.'

'It wasn't a difficult design. Pretty straightforward really, but I must admit I am pleased with it.'

'So you should be.' She reached up to grasp his face and plonked a kiss on his cheek.

'Muuum,' he whined, rubbing at the lipstick mark she'd left on his skin.

Julie chuckled. He'd always hated her doing that – which was why she did it. He was fun to wind up. She rarely bothered with lipstick anymore, but she'd worn some today to make Isaac believe she was getting her life back together. She'd fallen apart when Stephen had walked out and Isaac had been so worried about her that he'd left his house and his business in Wiltshire and had moved to be nearer to her, even though she'd protested that she didn't need him to keep an eye on her.

It was yet another thing to feel guilty about – never in a million years had she wanted to disrupt his life – but at least his business was picking up now and he'd reconnected with Nelly, so Julie didn't feel as bad as she might have done.

She saw Isaac glance at his watch again and she sighed. No doubt he had somewhere much more exciting to be, and she was just about to suggest that they get the key-collection over with when she noticed the contents of the welcome basket.

'Ooh, that's nice!' She picked up the bottle of wine and looked at the label. 'I'm going to enjoy that,' she said, opening the fridge and popping it inside.

'Is Petra planning on doing this for every rental, or is this a one off?'

'For every one,' he assured her. 'Come on, let's go. I'm meeting a client in an hour. A chap is thinking about building an eco-house, and I'd like to get the contract to draw up the plans.'

'Lead the way,' she said to him, hooking her coat over the newel post on the way out, and securing her bag more firmly on her shoulder. She might be okay with leaving her case in an unlocked house, but she certainly wasn't prepared to leave her handbag unattended. Anyone could walk in!

'I'm still a bit concerned about being stuck out here with no transport,' she said, as they walked towards the stables. She could see horses grazing in the fields, and sheep on the hillside above. It really was very rural.

A chicken scurried out from under a fence, making her jump, and she tightened her grip on her bag. If the creature tried to peck her, she'd swing her bag at it.

'I don't understand why you haven't bought yourself a little run-around.' Isaac flapped a hand at the hen to shoo it away.

The hen ignored him.

'It's on my to-do list,' she said, with a sigh. It was only fair that Stephen had the car when he left because he had to travel to work and often had loads of books to cart back and forth. She'd already taken early retirement and everything she needed, such as shops, the dentist and the doctor's surgery were within walking distance or a short bus-ride away if she was feeling lazy.

She'd been meaning to look for a little car, but she simply couldn't summon up the energy.

'You won't be stuck here,' Isaac said. 'Picklewick is two miles in that direction.' He pointed to the south. 'And there's a public right of way through the fields that will take you into the village. The forecast for the weekend is good, so it'll be a nice walk. You can have lunch there – I can heartily recommend the Black Horse, or there are a couple of cafes you could try. If you don't fancy that there are plenty of other walks you can go on, or you can just enjoy the peace and quiet and read. You could even have a riding lesson.'

'I don't think so!' The very idea made her shudder. She didn't mind horses – they were magnificent to look at – but she preferred to do that from a safe distance, not from the back of one of them.

As they neared the house, a wonderful smell of cooking assaulted her nostrils and Julie sniffed appreciatively.

'That smells good,' Isaac said. 'I wonder what Amos is cooking. Look, there's Petra, and she's got the baby with her.'

Julie saw a woman around the same age as Isaac, who was standing in the open doorway of an old farmhouse. She held a small baby in her arms, and the infant gazed around with wide curious eyes.

Her heart clenched when a memory of her younger self holding Isaac when he was a baby popped into her mind, and it was then Julie realised that her worries about staying in the cottage had nothing to do with prowlers or a lack of transport. The real reason was that she knew she was going to be lonely.

 Ha! Who was she kidding? She was already lonely and had been since Stephen had left her. At least this was a change of scenery, and being away from the house she'd lived in with Stephen might give her a chance to clear her head and decide what she was going to do with herself for the rest of her life.

'Hello,' the woman said, holding out a hand. 'I'm Petra and this is Amory. You must be Julie. Nice to meet you. I hope you enjoy your stay, but please let me know if there's anything you think we're not doing right.'

'Nice to meet you, too. And you, little one.' Julie gently stroked the baby's cheek. 'Don't worry, if I find anything I'll let you know, but I like what I've seen so far. The cottage is gorgeous and it's so welcoming.'

'Phew, that's a relief. You're the first person who hasn't been involved in the build to have seen it.'

'You've done a good job,' Julie said. 'I'm sure I won't find anything major.'

'I hope not. Come inside and I'll make a pot of tea. Amos, my uncle, has also made a cake – not the same one as in your welcome basket, so would you like a slice of that? Oh, and Isaac told us you don't have a car, so Amos has also made you a casserole for this evening, in case you didn't feel like venturing out.'

Julie was astonished. 'I don't know what to say – that's so kind of you.'

An older gentleman was taking the lid off a casserole dish, a wooden spoon in his hand, and she craned her neck to see what was in it. Whatever it was smelled delicious.

'Hang on, let me give this a quick stir,' Amos said. 'I hope you like lamb. We have an abundance of them around here.'

'Not goat?' she chuckled, and Amos looked horrified. 'Sorry, it was a joke,' she added hastily. 'I love lamb and that smells divine.'

'Please don't feel obliged to eat it,' he said, and he looked so concerned that Julie felt for him.

'Do you mind if I have a taste?' she asked.

'While you do that, I'll put the kettle on,' Petra said.

Julie said to Isaac, 'Do you have to get off?'

'I've got time to join you for a quick cuppa and see you settled into the cottage,' her son said, with a glance at Petra, who nodded.

She had nothing to do, apart from unpack her small case, and she had nowhere she needed to be, and Petra seemed lovely and so did Amos, so she was more than happy to stay for a little while, although she didn't want to impose.

Feeling better about the weekend already, she was suddenly glad that she'd agreed to this little break.

The stables on Muddypuddle Lane was easy enough to find. Just off the main road, up a narrow lane that was pitted with potholes which Stephen guessed would be full of muddy water when it rained, and there it was on the right.

Remembering Isaac's instructions, he drove past the little carpark that said "parking for riders only", and aimed for a single track which he'd been informed led to a parking area for the cottages.

It looks pretty enough, he thought, as he parked the car and got out. The cottages were in a row of three, identical apart from different coloured benches outside each one. Everything was spick and span, and as neat as a pin. He could tell that the landscaping around the building had only recently been done because the plants were small and not yet established, but it still looked lovely.

So far, first impressions were good. The only thing he could comment on was that the distance from the parking area to the cottages was about fifty metres, but he could see why the owners hadn't wanted people to park their vehicles directly in front of the houses, because...just look at that view!

It was rather impressive. From here Stephen could see right across the valley to the hills on the other side and everything in between. And if he craned his neck, he could just make out the turret of Picklewick's church in the distance.

He turned around to gaze up at the hillside above, seeing swathes of bracken and heather, and the occasional white blob of a sheep, and he realised he was really looking forward to exploring. Although he only lived ten or so miles away from Picklewick, he'd never really paid the village or the surrounding area much attention. Maybe after he'd unpacked and had a bite to eat, he'd put his hiking boots on and go for a walk. The views would be even more impressive from up there he thought, as he scanned the hillside, his eyes coming to rest on the swathes of bracken and heather on the open moorland above.

The door to the first cottage was unlocked, as expected, and Stephen carried his holdall inside. Then he hesitated.

A case was sitting at the foot of the stairs and a jacket was hanging on the bannister.

Was he in the correct cottage, he wondered?

Perplexed, he went back outside and tried the doors to the other two houses. Both were firmly locked.

He returned to the first cottage, and after dithering for a moment he ventured inside once more. This **must** be the right one.

 Stephen bit his lip, then took his phone out of his pocket.

Damn it, he'd forgotten Isaac had told him that he mightn't get any signal.

Slipping his mobile back into his pocket, he realised that the scene was probably staged. Isaac had explained that the owners were in the process of setting up a website and taking photos, so the case was probably to do with that.

Feeling somewhat happier, he went into the living room and came to another halt. This time it was because he liked what he saw, and after he'd taken it all in, he moved over to the table on which sat an old-fashioned wicker shopping basket. It contained a box of tea bags, a jar of coffee, and other things, and there was also a box beside it containing a bottle of gin: Isaac must have told Petra that he was partial to a G&T. It also held pasta and fresh veg, and when he went into the kitchen and saw a bottle of wine in the fridge, plus milk, butter and eggs, he was extremely impressed.

He hadn't got as far as thinking about dinner this evening, except for a vague idea that he might pop into Picklewick, but on seeing what the welcome pack entailed, he might not bother going out. He wasn't brilliant in the kitchen but he could rustle up a decent enough meal if he had to, and he could certainly do something with the pasta.

He couldn't see a set of keys anywhere, which was a bit troubling, but he decided to unpack first, then have a good look for them. And if he still couldn't see them, he'd go up to the main house and ask.

The upstairs of the cottage was just as nice as the downstairs he saw, as he stepped onto the landing. There were two good-sized bedrooms and both had en suites which consisted of a bath with a shower, and a loo.

Experimentally, Stephen turned on all the taps to check they worked, then tried the shower to make sure there was decent water pressure. After that, he flushed both loos and declared himself happy with the state of the plumbing.

Deciding he liked the front bedroom best with its sweeping views over the valley, he sat on the bed and gave the mattress an experimental bounce. Neither too firm nor too soft, and he was pleased to find that it didn't squeak. Not that it mattered to him, but a squeaky bed might be an issue for others.

Suddenly Stephen was acutely aware that he was here on his own. No significant other to share the bed with, no one to enjoy a meal with, or to enthuse with over the view.

But then again, he should be used to that by now. He hadn't had any of those things since Julie had confessed to having an affair, and it would probably be a long time before he had them again. Maybe never, because at the moment, despite telling himself that he should buck his ideas up, press on with getting a divorce and start enjoying life again, he simply couldn't bring himself to.

The only woman he'd ever wanted was Julie, and he couldn't see that changing anytime soon.

His heart feeling suddenly heavier, he trotted back downstairs to make himself a cup of tea and have a slice of cake. He'd feel better after a nice cuppa. He hoped.

Removing his jacket, he popped his car keys, wallet and mobile phone on the worktop, then set about making himself at home.

He swilled the kettle out, then filled it and plugged it in, and while he waited for it to boil, he opened the cupboards and peered inside. The kitchen was very well appointed, he admitted, taking a mug with a picture of a goat on it out of one of them and putting it next to the kettle.

It was while he was getting the milk out of the fridge that he heard the front door open, and he frowned. The owners must have guessed he was here because his car was in the parking space, so he wasn't happy about them walking in unannounced. Stephen was sure that was against the law or something. Surely, Petra, or whatever her name was, should have at least knocked first?

Stephen heard footsteps in the hall and turned to have a word with her. This wasn't a good start and he intended to—

'Julie!' He blinked in astonishment at the sight of his estranged wife standing in the doorway to the kitchen. Her mouth was open and she looked as shocked as he felt. She seemed to be holding a casserole dish with a tea towel wrapped around it, and for a second Stephen fixated on that, as he tried to work out what she was doing here.

When he eventually looked at her face, it was as white as the linen on the bed upstairs and her eyes were wide with shock.

She glanced behind her, and said, 'Isaac?'

'Hi, Dad.' Isaac waved at him from the doorway.

'What are you doing here?' Stephen looked at Julie, then back at his son. 'Isaac? What's going on?' He didn't need to ask – he'd already guessed, and he wasn't happy.

'Take me home, Isaac,' Julie demanded. 'I don't know what you're playing at, but it's not funny.'

'No,' Isaac said. 'I won't.'

'Fine, **I'll** go.' Stephen put the bottle of milk down on the worktop. He hadn't wanted to come here in the first place. Julie was welcome to it. He reached for his keys, irritation washing over him.

Isaac said, 'I don't think so,' and before Stephen realised what his son was doing, Isaac had scooped them up and was heading out of the door.

'Give those back!' he demanded, hurrying after him. 'Isaac! Give me my keys.'

Isaac ignored him and hotfooted it out of the house. By the time Stephen reached the door, Isaac was running up the path as though the hounds of hell were after him.

'Isaac!' Stephen yelled furiously. How dare he! He began to chase after him, but only managed a few steps before realising he didn't stand a hope in hell of catching him. 'Come back here this instant!' he shouted, using his best teacher voice.

It seemed to do the trick, because Isaac slowed down and turned around, but he didn't stop. Instead, he danced backwards, dangling Stephen's car keys, and called, 'You can thank me later.'

'Isaac!' Stephen thundered. 'Get back here **now**!'

'Enjoy your weekend,' Isaac shouted back. He had a huge grin on his face, which infuriated Stephen even more.

'I'll do no such thing!' he yelled. What on earth was Isaac thinking? Just wait until he got his hands on the boy!

'At least try.' Isaac was almost at the end of the path. 'It's an ideal opportunity for you and Mum to sort yourselves out. Bye!'

Then he was gone, leaving Stephen staring balefully after him.

'We'll see about that,' he muttered, and turned around, intending to go back inside to ring for a taxi.

It seemed that Julie had the same idea, because she was standing in the doorway, her mobile in her hand, frowning at it.

He watched as she held it above her head, moving it this way and that, and he guessed she was trying to get a signal.

Damn and blast, he'd forgotten about the patchy reception.

'I'm going to go back up to the house,' she said, not looking at him. 'I can't get a signal here. Petra can call a taxi for me.'

'You needn't go — I will,' he said crossly. He intended to give this Petra-woman a piece of his mind: she must be in on this outrageous plan of Isaac's, and he wasn't happy at all. How dare their son play such a stupid prank! What the hell did he think he was going to achieve?

Wordlessly, Julie shrugged, then plonked herself down on the bench outside the cottage. At least she was as shocked as he, Stephen thought. If she'd been in on it too, he'd have been even more annoyed.

He fetched his phone, and muttering darkly he headed up the path, giving his car a stern glare as he walked past. He'd go to the stables, where hopefully he'd find the owner.

However, the yard was deserted apart from a couple of chickens scratching about, and there was no answer to his shouted 'Hello.' He dithered for a moment then decided to try the house, but there was no answer to his insistent knocking, either. He debated whether to try the handle to see whether the door was unlocked, but thought better of it. As desperate as he was to get away from this place, he couldn't bring himself to enter a house without permission.

Sullenly, he backed away and peered through the nearest window, but he didn't see any sign of life. And he didn't have any more luck when he stuck his head into a barn, although he did have a bit of a shock when a goat bleated. The creature got up on its hind legs, it's front ones on the bars of its pen, and stared curiously. Another, smaller goat was in the pen with it, and it also stared at him. He'd never realised how odd looking their eyes were, and he shuddered.

'Shoo,' he said to them as he retreated, wincing as the goat's bleating followed him outside.

He scanned the yard once more and listened hard for signs of human activity, before giving in and returning to the cottage.

'I hope you ordered two taxis,' Julie said.

'I didn't order any,' he admitted. 'I couldn't find anyone.'

'Strange. Petra and Amos were there a few minutes ago.'

'We've been setup and the owners are in on it,' Stephen told her. Disbelief rode him hard. That Isaac should do such a thing when he knew what his mother had done and how Stephen felt about it, was inexcusable.

'What do we do now?' she asked. Julie seemed far less annoyed than he was. She was subdued and not in the least bit like her normal sparky self, and a worm of worry unfurled in his chest.

Stephen was struck by how wan she looked, and how drawn her face was. His wife had lost weight since he'd seen her last, and it didn't suit her. She'd never been robust and had always been slender, but now she looked positively gaunt, and he wondered whether she was eating properly.

An awful thought struck him.

Might she be ill?

She certainly didn't look well, so maybe she **was** unwell. He'd have thought Isaac would have mentioned it though, so he was probably overthinking it. Still, that worm of worry was now squirming around and making its presence felt.

'We've got a couple of options,' he said, thinking hard. 'We can wait until someone shows up and demand they phone a taxi for us. Or if we don't want to wait, I can take a stroll and find somewhere I can get a signal, or I can walk into Picklewick – I'll be sure to get one there. This isn't Timbuktu, for goodness' sake!' He stopped. There was a third option, one that he would never have considered if he hadn't seen her. 'Or we can make the best of it,' he said.

'Make the best of it?' Julie repeated woodenly.

'I don't know about you, but I could do with a few days away,' he found himself saying. 'Before the start of a new term...' He trailed off.

Her expression was unreadable. 'I thought you were going to retire?'

'Yes, well, things change.' What was the point of retiring when he didn't have anyone to enjoy all that free time with? Over the past few months his job had been the only thing to have got him out of bed some mornings.

Julie dropped her gaze and stared at the ground in front of her feet.

'We're two civilized people,' he carried on hurriedly, not wanting to rake everything up again. They'd said more than enough already. 'I'm sure we can co-exist in the same house for a few nights. It's not as though we'll have to share a bedroom.' As soon as the words left his mouth, he winced. He hadn't meant to sound so harsh.

She shot him a glance, and he saw two spots a colour bloom on her cheeks.

'That would be unthinkable,' she said, and he could have sworn there was a hint of sarcasm in her voice.

He let it slide. 'We can still be friends, can't we? After all, we have a son in common.'

Even as he said it, Stephen wasn't sure **friends** was the right word. They'd hardly spoken since he'd walked out after she'd dropped her bombshell, but the son part was right. If Isaac and Nelly carried on the way they were going, there could be wedding bells on the horizon and grandchildren. It would be good if he and Julie made an effort to get on. They could start the process here. And if they were at each other's throats come the morning, then one or the other could go home.

'You want us to stay here? Me and you, on our own?' Julie said.

Now that she put it that way, he wasn't so sure it was a good idea.

But before he could say anything else, she said, 'Okay, I'm game if you are. I wasn't looking forward to sleeping here on my own.' She blushed suddenly, the spots on her cheeks flaring into life to suffuse her face and neck with colour. 'That's not what I—'

Stephen leapt in. 'I know what you meant.' Good lord, this was going to be awkward. They were behaving like strangers, not like a couple who had been married for decades and who knew each other inside out.

Ha! But he **hadn't** known her as well as he'd thought he had, so maybe she **was** a stranger, after all.

Feeling that he'd made a mistake in suggesting they spend the weekend together but not wanting to back out now and look a pratt, Stephen did the only thing he could think of – he made a cup of tea.

CHAPTER THREE

Julie slowly unpacked her overnight case with trembling fingers. Stephen had carried it upstairs for her while the kettle boiled, putting it in the bedroom at the back of the cottage. His holdall already sat on the floor of the front bedroom, and she guessed he'd bagged that one for himself.

She hadn't brought much with her – a couple of changes of clothes, sturdy shoes for walking, her night things – so she was soon done, and was placing her toiletries bag in the en suite and feeling thankful that they didn't have to share a bathroom, when Stephen's voice floated up the stairs.

'Tea's ready.'

Gosh, this situation was totally unreal, and she wasn't sure how to deal with it. Never in a million years would she have thought she'd be spending a weekend with her husband. She'd assumed that he wanted nothing more to do with her – and he hadn't, not for many months. She'd not set eyes on him since he'd walked out, and she'd only had the briefest of conversations with him when he'd phoned to arrange to collect his things. He'd requested that she be out when he did, to avoid any awkwardness, and she'd obliged, not wanting to witness his grief first hand. Or his anger.

Stephen had been very angry and she didn't blame him. If she had discovered that **he'd** had an affair, she'd have been furious too, no matter how long ago it had taken place.

The olive branch he was now holding out was bittersweet.

She didn't know if she would be able to cope with them being friends, or whether it would be too much to bear. Still, she'd give it a go, for Isaac's sake if nothing else. Isaac...Hmm...She'd have a few choice words to say to her son the next time she saw him.

'Coming,' she called, rinsing her hands and wiping them on a large fluffy towel.

She checked her appearance in the mirror above the wash hand basin, and didn't particularly like what she saw. So in a vain attempt to look less ghoul-like, she pinched her cheeks to try to bring some colour into them.

Oh well, she reasoned, giving up on her appearance, Stephen had seen her in far worse states than this. Yet, as she went downstairs, she wished she'd made more of an effort. If she'd known she was going to see him, she'd have—

What? Had her hair done? Painted her toenails?

She found Stephen on the patio, a tray on the table. He was pouring tea from a proper teapot. It was in the shape of a horse and it brought a smile to her lips, as did the mugs which had pictures of various farm animals on them. His was a goat, hers was a sheep.

'Cake?' he asked, handing her a mug as she sat down.

'Yes, please.' She wasn't hungry, but she guessed she could do with the sugar because she was feeling decidedly shaky. 'Mmm,' she said, taking a bite. Amos was a good baker, which gave her hope for their dinner later. 'Amos has made us a casserole,' she told him, brushing cake crumbs off her lap. 'He's Petra's uncle.

Isaac says he owns the place. He made this cake, too.'

'It's nice, but it's not a patch on yours. Do you do much baking these days?'

'Not really.' She didn't do any baking at all. There seemed little point since she'd be the only one to eat it. In fact, she didn't do much in the way of cooking either, for the same reason.

Anyway, her appetite wasn't what it had been. If she did cook herself a meal, she found she'd only eat a few mouthfuls, then she'd lose interest. And she hated eating on her own, so she had resorted to taking a tray into the sitting room and eating in front of the TV. It was company of sorts, and by having the telly on she didn't feel so alone.

Unless Isaac was joining her – then she'd make a show of cooking a decent meal, so he didn't worry. However, now that he had Nelly, Julie was seeing less of him at mealtimes, and as a consequence her food intake had taken a hit as she tended to snack only when she was hungry and didn't bother with three square meals a day.

'I used to love your upside-down cake,' Stephen said. 'And your scones. You used to make a mean cream tea.'

'I suppose I still could if I put my mind to it.'

'You mentioned a casserole?'

'Yes. Amos made it, in case I didn't want to venture out. I assumed it was because they knew I wouldn't have any transport.' She gave him a meaningful look.

'Anyone would think this had been planned all along,' Stephen said. He was staring at the hillside above the cottage, so she took the opportunity to stare at him. He'd lost some weight, she noticed, and she wondered whether he wasn't eating properly either. He was a decent enough cook, and when she'd been working full-time they'd shared kitchen duties. He looked well though, so maybe he'd been on a health-kick.

A thought stopped her in her tracks. Maybe he'd been working out, getting himself all thin and ship-shape for another woman?

Isaac hadn't mentioned that his father was dating, but perhaps that was what this subterfuge was about – a last-ditch attempt by Isaac at a reconciliation between his parents before Stephen fell in love with someone else.

Julie was surprised that Stephen hadn't told her he wanted a divorce. She'd been expecting it ever since he'd left, and every time a letter landed on the mat her heart had been in her mouth.

It was the next step. She knew they couldn't continue in this limbo for ever.

Sooner or later, they'd have to sever this last tie.

Her gaze dropped to his left hand, and she noticed with a twinge that he no longer wore his wedding ring. She still wore hers. She'd removed her engagement ring and her diamond eternity ring, but she hadn't been able to bring herself to take her wedding ring off.

Stephen let out a sigh. 'So, here we are.' He sounded as nonplussed about the situation as she felt.

'Yes, here we are,' she agreed. She tried to smile, but she guessed it was more of a grimace.

'I think I'll go for a walk,' he said. 'Explore a bit.'

'Good idea.' A couple of hours of not being in his company might go some way to settle her ragged nerves. On the other hand, she might spend them fretting about his return.

This wasn't going to work, was it? They'd not spoken in months and now Isaac expected them to spend the weekend together.

'Would you like to join me?' he asked.

'Pardon?'

'I was thinking we could go for a walk, but if you don't—'

'I'd like that.' She'd spoken without thinking, her heart leaping at the chance before her brain could protest. 'I'll just change my shoes,' she said, getting to her feet and collecting up the tea things.

'I'll do that,' Stephen said. 'You go and get ready.'

Julie was glad of a few moments alone. What on earth had possessed her to agree to go for a walk with him? She'd already concluded that this weekend wouldn't work, yet here she was, shoving her feet into a pair of trainers, her heart hammering with anticipation at the thought of being in his company. She must be mad to put herself through such torture. He was clearly only trying to make the best of it for Isaac's sake. If she wasn't careful she'd have her already broken heart shattered into a million pieces, and she had a feeling that if she suffered any more heartache, she wouldn't ever recover from it.

'Psst, Harry, come here.' Petra beckoned him over to the window. She was peering out of it, feeling quite smug.

Harry had only just returned to the stables after a day of blacksmithing and the first thing he'd done was to pick Amory up and give him a cuddle. 'What is it?' he asked, lumbering to his feet, the baby in his arms.

'Look.' She pointed to the middle-aged couple walking down the path towards the cottages. 'That's Isaac's parents. They've been out for a walk. I watched them leave.'

'And now they've returned.' Harry's voice was dry. 'What's for supper?'

'Um, lamb casserole. Amos made two, one for us and one for them. They're talking to each other, see?'

'So?'

Petra sighed, irritated at his lack of interest in what she thought was an absorbing topic. He hadn't appeared too interested when she'd initially told him about Isaac's plan either. 'Isaac's dad, Stephen, came up to the house earlier. Isaac warned me he might do that. He didn't look happy and kept staring at his phone. So we hid upstairs.'

'We?'

'Me, Amos and the baby.'

Harry shook his head. 'I'm glad I wasn't here. What if he comes back?'

'I doubt if he will.' Petra sounded more confident than she felt, but at least the pair were talking to each other, so that was a start. 'If he wanted to leave, he could have walked into Picklewick, or got a signal while they were on their walk,' she added.

 'He could have got a signal in the yard,' Harry pointed out.

Petra was glad Stephen hadn't realised. 'I hope Isaac's plan works, and they get back together.'

'I hope they give us a good report on the cottage,' Harry retorted, giving her a meaningful look. The couple were now out of sight, and he drew away from the window. 'Are you still going dress shopping tomorrow?' he asked.

Petra pulled a face. 'I suppose.'

'You don't have to,' Harry told her. He juggled the baby onto his shoulder, holding Amory firmly with one hand, and put the other around Petra's waist.

In a teasing voice she said, 'Now that you come to mention it, I have seen a pair of white wellies with a ribbon on them. I could wear them with white jodhpurs.' Actually, that did sound rather fetching.

'If you want to wear jodhpurs, wear them,' he said. 'You'll look beautiful regardless. Besides, what you wear isn't important; what's important is that we're getting married.'

'Aw, do you know how much I love you?'

'Enough to ask Amos when supper will be ready? I'm starving.'

'You're such a romantic,' she said, kissing him on the cheek. She was so lucky to have found him, and although she wasn't too keen on all the weddingy fuss, she couldn't wait to be his wife.

As she leant into him, she smiled to herself, remembering the first time she'd set eyes on him. Never would she have guessed that she'd fall in love with him and they would create such a gorgeous child together!

'I'll warm the casserole up in the oven,' Julie said to Stephen as he took it out of the fridge. 'It'll be nicer than in the microwave.'

She held her hands out and he passed the dish to her, but as he did so his fingers brushed against hers and he almost leapt out of his skin.

'Careful,' she said, as he fumbled the hand-over. 'It would be a shame to drop it. It looks delicious.'

Stephen couldn't care less about their dinner. He was too busy thinking about his reaction to that fleeting contact. He'd felt such a surge of desire, it had taken his breath away.

Heart thudding, he turned back to the fridge and reached for the bottle of gin. He could seriously do with a drink or two, after the day he'd had.

Without asking whether Julie wanted one, he poured the drinks, being careful to place her glass on the worktop. He didn't want to risk touching her again in case he did something silly.

The problem was, this afternoon had been like old times and it had stirred up too many memories and emotions. He'd known that he wasn't over her and he guessed he probably never would be, although for these past few months he'd managed to bury his feelings deep enough to be able to function without falling apart. But this afternoon had brought all of the love and the heartache rushing back to the surface, until he was barely holding himself together.

The initial awkwardness as they had begun their walk had gradually given way to a more comfortable atmosphere, and by the time they'd hiked onto the moorland above the fields neither of them had much breath to spare for talking, having to use all their energy to climb ever upwards. And on reaching the top the view had taken whatever breath they had left.

All the while though, he'd been acutely aware of Julie by his side, of every step she took and every sound she made, and he'd longed to take her in his arms and beg her to tell him that she loved him.

His heart ached as he remembered how easily she'd spoken those three little words in the past, and it bled as he wondered whether she had ever meant them.

Taking a gulp of gin and tonic, he wandered onto the terrace and slumped into a chair.

This was such a mistake. He should have left while he had the chance, before the walls that he'd so carefully built around his heart were destroyed. He could already feel them crumbling and if they fell he didn't know how he'd be able to carry on. Because the short amount of time that he'd spent with his wife this afternoon confirmed what he'd already feared – he still loved her, totally and utterly, and the thought of spending the rest of his life without her filled him with despair.

Thankfully Julie had turned the radio on in the kitchen, so at least there was some noise to alleviate the tension. He didn't know whether she could feel it too, or whether it was his imagination, but he could have sworn it filled the very air, as real as the song that was blaring cheerfully from the speakers.

He snorted to himself – Petra really had thought of everything. He'd make sure to add to his notes that the radio was a nice touch.

'Sit yourself down, it's almost ready,' Julie said, appearing on the patio, and he felt a pang of guilt that he hadn't helped her prepare the meal.

Not that there had been a lot of preparation to be done, but at least he could have helped lay the table or something. After all, she was here to have a break just like he was. She wasn't here to wait on him and neither would he want her to. It would be far too reminiscent of when they used to live together. He hadn't expected to be waited on then, but after she'd taken early retirement and he was still working, she'd insisted on doing everything around the house. Which he'd appreciated, because teaching wasn't an 8:30 to 3:30 profession. Just because school ended mid-afternoon, didn't mean he was free to leave at that time. He often ran after school clubs, mainly aimed at the examination classes, and there were always meetings to attend and training sessions to be sat through. Not only that, there was all the paperwork that teachers were expected to complete, as well as the necessary lesson preparation and marking.

But right now, he didn't want to feel beholden to her, even for something as simple as reheating a casserole. Sharing a meal with her felt even more intimate than that brief touch of fingers earlier. He vividly remembered the last time they had sat down to eat together, because that had been the day Julie had blown his world apart.

He'd known there was something wrong the second he'd walked in from work, but he hadn't been able to put his finger on it.

She'd looked as though she'd been crying and her face had been flushed, but when he'd asked her if she was okay, she'd blamed it on the menopause, and he knew she still suffered from it so he took it at face value. Although he distinctly remembered feeling a frizzle of unease as he'd taken the pile of books he had been carrying up to the spare room which he'd turned into an office. It wasn't until her face had crumbled over her bowl of chicken noodles had he realised something was very wrong indeed.

It had all come out. How could it not when she had been in so much distress? She'd been distraught: he couldn't ever remember seeing her as grief stricken. Not even when her mum had passed on, had she broken down like that.

His own grief was swift to follow when he'd realised what she was telling him. She had loved someone else. Loved them enough to consider leaving him, and it was only because she had been pregnant that she hadn't.

He'd shouted, he'd cried, there had been recriminations and accusations, but at least he'd never doubted that Isaac was his, because if the boy hadn't been, Julie would have walked out of their marriage.

Stephen supposed he should be thankful that she **hadn**'t left him, that she had allowed him the joy of seeing his son grow up, and had allowed him to be a father to Isaac. She could so very easily have lied to both him and Emrys, and claimed that Isaac was Emrys's son. If she had done, she could have followed her heart. But she hadn't. She'd stayed with him, and all this time he'd been oblivious to the pain she was hiding. He'd also been oblivious to the fact that she hadn't loved him as much as he'd loved her.

Although he might be thankful that she hadn't left, he couldn't bring himself to forgive her for her betrayal. No matter how deeply he still loved her, how much he missed her, or how little his life was worth living without her, forgiveness was beyond him.

So why was he here?

He'd been asking himself that very question ever since he'd suggested they spend the weekend together. He tried to justify it by claiming it was for Isaac's sake, but he was lying. It was for his own sake. He so desperately wanted to be with her because he wanted, however briefly, to remember what it was like being married to her.

Then he snorted to himself as he thought how ridiculous he was being. He was **still**

married to her, despite feeling that they should get a divorce.

He honestly didn't think he could bring himself to start the ball rolling. What was the point? It might sever their ties completely, but that didn't mean to say he was going to move on. His half-baked idea about putting himself back out there, back on the dating scene, was a ridiculous notion. He knew he wouldn't, no matter how lonely he felt. He simply couldn't face having any other woman in his life.

Julie put a plate laden with food in front of him and he looked up. 'Thanks,' he said, giving her a small smile. 'It smells divine.'

'It does, doesn't it?' she agreed, slipping into the seat opposite with her own plate in her hands. He noticed that she had about half of the amount of food on hers that he had on his.

'Are you trying to fatten me up?' he asked.

'Not at all, although you have lost some weight. You're looking good.'

It was more than he could say for her. She was still beautiful, but her beauty now had an ethereal quality. Her skin was like porcelain, and he worried that she might break.

'You know what it's like,' he said. 'I'm too busy to eat some days.' Stephen was making excuses. He wasn't too busy at all: he just couldn't be bothered. Cooking for himself wasn't something that appealed to him, and neither was eating a meal alone, so during term time he usually ate in the school canteen, surrounded by hundreds of shouting children and the pained faces of his colleagues as they tried to ignore the noise. The food wasn't exactly gourmet and he did try to choose a healthy option, but despite the Healthy Schools Initiative, the food tended to be full of stodge. The only thing that counteracted the excessive amount of carbs, was the fact that the portions were small.

Very often when he got in from work, he didn't bother with a meal, he just snacked. He knew he'd lost weight over the course of the summer holidays, because he hadn't had a school cafeteria to visit and neither had he wanted to go anywhere such as a pub or cafe to eat. The thought of sitting there on his own filled him with despair, so over the past five weeks he'd been living on a selection of sandwiches, tins of soup and the occasional frozen meal. It probably hadn't helped that he didn't have much of an appetite.

'How about you? You seem to have lost weight, too,' he pointed out.

'Well, you know what it's like,' she echoed, then trailed off and smiled at him.

The smile was sad and uncertain, and he saw the despair behind it. She was still grieving for Emrys, and despite his own misery his heart went out to her.

They ate the meal without speaking, allowing the music to flow over them and the chatter of the radio presenter to fill the dead spaces between them. Stephen ate without tasting, although he did acknowledge that the casserole really was rather delicious, but after the first forkful he was on automatic pilot, simply chewing each mouthful with grim determination.

He was surprised, however, when he saw that he had cleared his plate, and he pushed it away feeling replete. Julie, he noticed, had hardly touched hers.

'What's wrong with your dinner?' he asked.

'I'm not hungry,' she replied, putting her knife and fork down neatly.

He blurted, 'Would you have eaten more if I hadn't been here?'

Her smile was still sad. 'I doubt it.'

It was none of his business – **she** was none of his business – but he found himself saying, 'You can't go on like this, you'll fade away.'

She didn't say anything for a moment, then she muttered, 'What do you care?'

Stephen frowned. 'It might surprise you to know that I do still care about you. I worry about you.'

'Do you?' She stared at him expressionlessly.

He pursed his lips. 'You can't be married to someone for as long as we were married, without still caring about them.'

She looked up and away, blinking
furiously, as her eyes filled with tears.

Dear god, please don't let her cry, he
pleaded silently. It would be his undoing.
Julie had never been a crier. Over the
years he'd seen her cry maybe less than a
dozen times. And one of those times had
been the day she'd informed him that
she'd been unfaithful. She'd cried some
more a day later, when he'd walked out
on his marriage.

He couldn't stand to see her cry, even if
the tears weren't for him.

'You've got a funny way of showing it,'
she said with a gulp.

He shrugged and took a deep breath,
then let it out slowly. What could he say
to that?

She fanned her face. 'I miss you,' she said
quietly.

The admission took him by surprise. 'Is that why you're crying?' He knew he was being sarcastic but he couldn't help himself.

'Actually, it is.'

Stephen hadn't been expecting that. He'd assumed the tears were for Emrys.

'I miss you too,' he said, and her eyes shot to his and he saw a flicker of...was that **hope**, in her face? 'But it's too late,' he continued, and the flicker dimmed.

'I know.' She stared at the table. Then abruptly she shoved her chair away and scrambled to her feet. 'I think I'll turn in,' she said, and he watched her dash out of the room and heard her feet on the stairs and then on the floorboards overhead, and he let out a deep sigh.

'Isaac,' he muttered, 'What the hell were you thinking?

Stephen couldn't blame the boy for trying, but neither could he thank him for it. This weekend was doing neither him nor Julie any good, and they hadn't even been here a day yet.

With another sigh, he rose and collected the plates. It was early, not quite eight o'clock, and he wasn't ready for bed. If the truth be known, he wasn't sleeping too well these days, and he didn't fancy going upstairs just to lie awake for hour after hour, especially with his wife in the room next door, only a short landing separating the two bedrooms.

Instead, after he washed up, he put his hiking boots back on and went out for another walk. If nothing else the exercise would do him good and he might be able to clear his head. Anything was better than lying there, wishing that things were different.

CHAPTER FOUR

Julie woke with a start, and it took her a moment to realise where she was. Abruptly she sat up and listened for any signs of life, but she heard nothing apart from the birds tweeting outside her window this morning, so she sank back down onto the pillows.

After she'd gone upstairs she'd heard the front door close, and she'd sneaked into the front bedroom and peeped through the curtains to see Stephen striding off in the same direction they had taken this afternoon. She couldn't be entirely certain, but she didn't think he was leaving. He didn't have his holdall with him for one thing, and neither was he going in the direction of Picklewick. However, he might well be searching for a place where he could get a phone signal so he could ring for a taxi.

Julie hadn't gone to bed to sleep last night: she'd gone to bed early to escape from Stephen. However, she hadn't been able to escape her feelings, and she'd lain there with tears trickling down her cheeks for quite some time, until she'd managed to pull herself together and the sobbing had turned to sniffling. At some point she must have drifted off to sleep, long after it had grown dark, but she still hadn't heard him come in, so this morning she was none the wiser as to whether he'd spent the night in the cottage or not.

A noise from downstairs made her sit up again, and she listened intently. There was a tinkle of what she thought might be cutlery, and she wondered whether

Stephen was downstairs making himself breakfast.

She eased out of bed as quietly as she could and padded to the bathroom, where she stared grimly at herself in the mirror, not liking what she saw. She had bags under her eyes bigger than the suitcase she'd brought with her, and her face was worryingly pale. She really must get out in the sunshine and the fresh air more, so at least she wouldn't look as though she was about to pop her clogs. No wonder Isaac worried about her.

After splashing her face with cold water and brushing her teeth, she dragged a comb through her hair and attempted to put on some makeup. A little blusher wouldn't go amiss, and neither would a sweep of mascara. She didn't bother with lipstick, because she needed a cup of tea and she'd only end up licking it all off, so instead she bit her lips, nibbling at them to try to make them look a little more pink. Satisfied that this was the best she could do for the time being, she got dressed and went downstairs.

Stephen was out on the terrace, which seemed to be his favourite place in the cottage, and when he heard her come into the living room he got to his feet.

'Would you like a cup of tea?' he asked.

'I'd love one, please.'

'How about some breakfast?'

'No, thanks, not just yet. I'll have tea first and see what I feel like later.'

'You must eat something,' her husband insisted. 'There's nothing left of you.'

'I eat when I'm hungry,' she said, eliciting a snort from him.

'Clearly you need to be hungry a little more often,' he shot back at her.

She took a seat and tilted her face up to the sun. Five minutes basking in its rays wasn't going to bring much colour to her face, but every little bit helped, she reasoned.

'Thanks,' she said, when he placed a cup of tea in front of her on the table.

'How did you sleep?' He was gazing at her with concern, and once more she felt tears perilously close to the surface.

'It took me a while to get off,' she admitted, 'but when I did I slept like the dead—' She stopped suddenly, and he made a face. 'How about you?' she asked.

'After you went to bed I went for a walk,' he said. 'I didn't get back until after dark.'

'Where did you go?'

'Back up onto the hill. I needed some time to think.'

'What about?'

'Us.'

'And?' Good grief this was worse than pulling teeth.

'We can't go on like this,' he began.

'I know,' she said softly. 'What do you suggest?'

'I don't honestly know.'

Her voice was even quieter when she said, 'Do you want to get a divorce?' and she was gratified when he shot her a horrified look.

'No, I don't. I have thought about it,' he admitted, 'but is there any point?'

'You said yourself that we can't go on like this,' she replied.

He said, 'Divorce or not, we'll still be in the same situation, won't we? Living in separate houses, leading separate lives.'

'We don't have to make any decisions right now,' she pointed out. 'In the scheme of things, it's still early days.'

'It feels like forever,' Stephen said. He also had bags under his eyes, and didn't look as though he'd slept very well. He looked better than she did though, she conceded.

'Yes, it does,' she agreed quietly. It felt like they'd been apart for years, not months.

They sat in silence for a while, Stephen staring into the distance, Julie sipping her tea and watching him out of the corner of her eye.

'I'm going to make some sandwiches,' he announced, getting to his feet.

'Isn't it early for a sandwich'? she asked.

'I think we should go exploring and take a picnic with us.'

'More walking? Didn't you do enough yesterday?'

'You don't have to come if you don't want to,' he told her.

'I'd like to come. Where were you thinking of going?' Even as she asked the question, she knew deep down what his reply would be and her heart sank.

'How about if we head over that way?' He pointed to a track running parallel to the road. A little way long that track she knew she'd be able to see a certain layby.

She briefly thought about suggesting another direction, then she realised it was futile; she couldn't run away from Emrys, because he was in her heart. She had carried him there for all this time and she couldn't dislodge him now, and neither did she want to. He was as much a part of her as Stephen, so did it matter if they took the path above the road where she used to meet him?

'That sounds lovely,' she said, meaning it. In fact, it seemed fitting that she, Stephen and Emrys would all be in the same place. Emrys might not be there in body, but he'd be there in spirit. It was time to reconcile the three parts of herself, and maybe, just maybe she might begin to feel whole once more.

'Come on, Petra, there must be something you like,' Charity said. 'How about this one?' She held up a blush pink dress that looked more like a ball gown than a wedding dress. Petra thought it was too low cut and a bit flouncy, all chiffon and layers. She'd look like a silly doll in it.

Crossly, she shook her head. She was seriously getting to the end of her tether. She had never liked shopping, unless it was for horsey stuff. Thankfully Amos did all the food shopping, so she was spared that weekly chore, and she'd had her fill of shopping lately, when she'd kitted out the three cottages. She was all shopped out. Even if she hadn't been, she hated shopping for clothes. She had no idea what suited her, but it certainly wasn't any of the dresses she'd seen on the rails today.

She could tell that Charity, October and Megan were starting to become a little exasperated. They weren't the only ones – she was exasperated, too. She supposed it served her right to leave buying a wedding dress until the last minute.

To her shock, the staff in the first bridal shop they'd tried had been rather sniffy with her. Apparently they only stocked sample dresses that were just meant to be tried on and not bought there and then. She had been informed that if she liked one of the dresses then they would order it in in her size and she could have it altered if necessary. When Petra explained that she needed it for two weeks today, she was met with a horrified gasp and a hushed exclamation of how that time scale simply wasn't feasible. The standard lead time was eight to ten **months**.

Petra wasn't too bothered, because she hadn't seen anything she really liked anyway. Nothing was **her**. Although she wasn't actually sure what was **her,** when it came to dresses. She couldn't remember the last time she'd worn one. Possibly when she went to the prom when she finished school? Hang on, no, she hadn't worn a dress then, either. She'd worn what was commonly referred to as a playsuit, an all-in-one outfit with wide pant legs and a fitted bodice with little straps. She'd been sixteen and able to get away with wearing that kind of thing. She'd look ridiculous if she attempted to wear something similar these days.

Petra and her entourage were met with the same reaction by the staff in the next shop they went into, and by this time October and Charity were holding hushed conversations about how important it was to plan weddings well in advance. After the third shop, they retreated to a rather large department store, and were now rooting around in the ballgown section.

Blush pink indeed! Petra snorted. She wasn't a blush pink woman. Anyway, although Harry had said he didn't mind what colour dress she wore, she guessed he'd be disappointed if it wasn't white, or at least cream. White didn't suit her complexion, but she could possibly manage ivory or cream. Unfortunately, there weren't a great many dresses in this shop that were even remotely suitable in that colour.

Megan held up a sheath dress with a diamante effect around the waist. 'How about this?'

Petra wrinkled her nose. It was plain enough, apart from that silly bit of decoration, but she wasn't sure about the style. Pre-baby she would probably have got away with it, but not post-Amory. Even though she hadn't put on a great deal of weight when she was pregnant and it had now come off thanks to all the riding she did plus breastfeeding, her figure had changed nevertheless and she didn't think it was for the better.

At least this marathon dress-hunt was showing her what she did and didn't like, so there was that. But unfortunately, she had to buy something today or be forced to return again next weekend when she would be under even more pressure to buy something.

'Right,' Megan said, taking charge. 'You sit there.' She put her hands on Petra's shoulders and forced her into a chair. Petra wasn't sure the chair was meant for sitting on and was just for decoration, but she obediently sat anyway, wondering what was going to happen.

'The three of us...' Megan pointed to herself and the other two bridesmaids, 'are going to get you a selection of dresses and you're going to try them on.'

Petra stared at them. She didn't like the sound of that. So far she'd actually managed to avoid trying anything on at all.

'You won't know until you try something,' October urged, and Charity nodded vigorously.

'You'd be surprised,' Charity added. 'You might think something doesn't suit you or you don't like it, but when you get it on you realise that it's actually perfect.'

Petra didn't think that was likely to happen, but she decided to go along with it anyway. What choice did she have? And as she hadn't seen anything she liked yet, she might as well give this a go.

She waited impatiently for her maid-of-honour and her bridesmaids to return, and as she sat there she fretted that Nathan was okay. He'd taken a hack out this morning, to free her up to come shopping, and although he'd mellowed since he and Megan had got together, he was still a taciturn man who much preferred horses and tractors to people, so wasn't the best front-man for the stables.

Petra smiled to herself, thinking that neither was she, if she was honest. She was well aware that she didn't suffer fools gladly, but her regular clients knew that and accepted her anyway. All that mattered to them was that she was a good riding instructor, although some of the mums of her young pupils would probably appreciate it if she had a more client-focused approach.

Petra tapped her foot, wondering how much longer this was going to take. They'd arrived in town at nine o'clock on the dot, ready for the shops to open, and it was now eleven-thirty. Amory would need feeding soon, and she had to get back for a lesson at four. She was getting hungry too, and could really do with a cup of coffee. Or maybe something stronger?

'Ta da!' The three would-be stylists leapt out from behind a rail and held up an assortment of dresses.

Petra stared at them in dismay before slowly closing her eyes and opening them again. God help her, but she just might wear jodhpurs and wellies after all.

'There's something very endearing about a donkey,' his wife said, as Stephen reached over the half-door of the stall to scratch between the animal's long ears. He thought she was right – donkeys were rather sweet.

They were on their way back from their walk, having been out all day, and had heard braying coming from the stable block, and Julie had insisted they investigate.

'Stay there,' she instructed. 'I want to take a photo.' She took her phone out of her jeans pocket and aimed it at him. 'Guess what?' she said, after she'd taken the photo. 'I've got a signal.'

Stephen's mouth twisted into a wry grin. 'It's lucky I didn't know I could get a signal here yesterday,' he said, 'otherwise I'd have phoned for that taxi.' He sobered. 'I've enjoyed today.'

'Me, too. I've got an awful feeling I'll ache like the devil tomorrow though. I can't remember the last time I did so much walking.'

It had been rather lovely. For whole stretches of time Stephen had forgotten they weren't together anymore, and they'd fallen into the easy way that they used to have.

Then he'd remember and would feel awkward for a while, but it soon passed as his attention was taken by the wonderful scenery.

At the start of their walk, they'd headed across county, along a path well used by horses from the look of all the hoof prints. It ran parallel to the road below, separated from it by lush green fields on which several horses grazed, one of whom had a foal.

Stephen had pointed it out to Julie, but she'd seemed lost in thought, and he'd begun to wonder whether it was a good idea to spend all day in her company if she was going to be morose. After a while she'd cheered up though, and he'd even go as far as to say she'd blossomed, and by the time they'd sat down beside a babbling stream to eat their picnic, Stephen was suddenly glad Isaac had forced them to come on this weekend away.

If their son's plan was for him and Julie to get back together, it wasn't going to work. But if Isaac's intent was for them to be able to be in the same room without awkwardness and tension, then he'd done a good job. Stephen felt confident that should Isaac and Nelly's relationship progress, he and Julie could play their parts as parents of the groom very amicably indeed.

However, every now and again Stephen had caught his wife's eye and he'd had to hastily look away, because he'd had a sudden urge to take her in his arms and kiss her. Or he'd brush against her, or she him, and a bolt of desire would shoot through him.

Along with the attraction he still felt for her (to him she would always be beautiful and incredibly sexy), were other emotions – love, longing and regret. He hadn't stopped loving her, and he longed for things to return to the way they'd been this time last year, when he'd been blissfully ignorant of the bombshell she would shortly drop on him. But he knew they never could.

A clatter of hooves brought him out of his thoughts, and he looked towards the noise.

Several ponies were being led out of a barn and were heading their way.

'Hi,' a young woman in her early thirties said. She handed over the reins of the pony she was leading to a girl of about eight or nine. 'Heidi, can you pop Parsnip into his usual stall and give him a brush down? You can put Tango in with him if you want. I'll be along in a minute.' The woman turned back to him and Julie. 'I see you've found Gerald. He'll let you do that all day.'

Stephen was still scratching between the animal's ears, and the donkey's eyes were almost closed in bliss.

'How are you finding the cottage?' she asked. 'I'm Petra, by the way.' This last bit was addressed to him, as Julie had met her yesterday.

'Nice to meet you,' he said, wondering how much of a part she'd played in setting him and Julie up. He didn't think she was entirely innocent.

'It's lovely,' Julie gushed. 'I honestly can't find fault with it.'

'Wifi might be a good idea,' he said, tongue-in-cheek, and Petra chuckled.

'Not having wifi is one of the selling points,' she told him, 'so you can get away from it all. What have you been up to today?'

'We went for a really long walk. The scenery around here is stunning, isn't it? Lots of little valleys with streams running through them – we had a picnic by one – and the open moorland with all that heather and bracken, and those glorious views,' Julie said.

'We found an old building right on the top. Did someone used to live there?' Stephen asked.

'It's an old farmhouse,' Petra explained, then chuckled. 'Perhaps I ought to do it up – it would be the ultimate get-away-from-it-all holiday.'

'You can say that again! It took us a couple of hours to get there on foot, and I'm not sure I'd want to be that secluded,' Julie said, and Stephen agreed with her.

'Maybe not,' Petra laughed. 'Anyway, it doesn't belong to the stables. It's on common land, but I believe it's part of the farm at the top of Muddypuddle Lane. Right, I'd best get on. I'm so pleased you are enjoying your stay, but do let me know if you can think of anything we should or shouldn't be doing.' She was about to walk off when she stopped. 'Oh, if you're interested, there's a fete on in Picklewick tomorrow. It should be good fun. I can drive you into the village, if you like?'

Ah ha! He thought. Gotcha! Petra was definitely in on this scheme of Isaac's. He narrowed his eyes at her, but before he could say anything, she added, 'It's probably best not to take your car, because parking will be a nightmare and there are so many lovely food and drink stalls, that you might want to indulge in a tipple or two.' Her smile was wide and innocent, and Stephen pursed his lips.

'It's okay, we can walk,' Julie said. 'But thanks for the offer.'

'I thought you said you didn't want to do anymore walking,' he said to her, once Petra was out of earshot.

'I don't,' his wife told him, 'but she's got a new baby, a business to run, and a wedding in a couple of weeks. I think she's got enough on her plate without taxiing us around.'

'I didn't realise. You're right, of course. Besides, the village isn't far.' He gave the donkey a final pat. 'Fancy pasta for dinner? I noticed you brought some with you. Then I thought we could have a quiet drink in the garden. Unless you've got other plans?'

'No, no plans. I'll cook; you made the picnic. But first, I need a long shower.'

'Good idea. I'll join you,' he said without thinking, and winced when she stared at him in shock. 'I mean,' he added hastily, 'that I'll also need to freshen up before we eat.'

'Yes, of course. I realised that...I didn't think you...I knew you meant...' She sighed, and changed the subject. 'Would you like tomato sauce, or creamy mushroom with the pasta?' And with that, the easy-going atmosphere was gone, and they were back to walking on eggshells again.

Stephen felt like kicking himself.

CHAPTER FIVE

'Did you get anything?' Amos asked, and Petra wrinkled her nose.

'Yes and no.'

'Nothing is ever straight forward with you, is it?' her uncle said fondly, as he grabbed the toast before the over-zealous toaster shot the bread halfway across the room.

Harry, who was nursing Amory whilst trying to eat a bowl of cereal, barked out a laugh. 'You should have seen her face when she showed it to me last night. Anyone would think she'd had to choose a dress to wear to the gallows, not for a wedding.'

Petra gave him the stink-eye. 'It's the best of a bad bunch,' she said. It was white, but that was about all the dress had going for it. It looked more like a nightie than a wedding gown, but at least it fitted and wasn't that awful shiny material that highlighted every bump and lump.

'What's wrong with it?' Amos wanted to know.

'What's right with it,' Petra muttered, buttering one of the pieces of toast and biting into it.

'Why did you buy it if you don't like it?' Amos's question was reasonable, but Petra wasn't in the mood to be reasonable.

'Because there are now only thirteen days to the wedding and everyone—' she shot Harry a filthy look so he was in no doubt that she was referring to him '—expects me to wear a dress.'

'I've told you, you can wear what you like,' Harry replied mildly.

'I thought it was bad luck for the groom to see the dress before the wedding?' Amos said.

'I wanted a second opinion.' Petra took another bite of her toast.

'Didn't you get one from Megan? And a third from October, and a fourth from Charity?' Amos raised his eyebrows.

'Ha, ha, very funny.' Petra scowled back.

'If you've shown it to Harry, you might as well show it to me,' Amos said.

'Can you take Amory?' Harry asked her. 'I've got stuff to do.'

'What stuff?' Petra wanted to know. 'It's Sunday, surely you aren't working today?'

'Oh, I, er, won't be long. I've got a Shire to look at. Split hoof.' Hurriedly he passed the baby to her and was gone before Petra had a chance to quiz him further.

She glared after him with narrowed eyes. He was up to something and she guessed it might be wedding related, and prayed he wasn't going to do anything outrageous. All she wanted was a quiet ceremony in the church, then return to the stables for a small glass of bubbly.

But the ceremony was growing – having a maid-of-honour and two bridesmaids ensured that – and she had a feeling that Harry and Amos were planning more than just a bite to eat and a bottle of plonk.

'What's he up to?' she asked, and when Amos shook his head in wide-eyed innocence and said, 'Nothing, why?' she knew he most definitely was.

'He'd better not be planning a fuss,' she warned.

'I'm sure he's not,' her uncle said.

Petra wasn't.

Amos said, 'Can you hold the ladder? I want to go up the attic.'

'Whatever for?'

'Just you wait and see.'

Petra followed him upstairs and put Amory in his cot, winding up the mobile hanging above it to try to keep the baby amused for a few minutes. Her son thought it was his right to be held constantly and was rather averse to being ignored.

Praying he wouldn't start bawling, she slipped out of his bedroom to find Amos opening the hatch to the attic and easing the folding ladder down. 'Would you like me to go up?' she offered.

'No.' His reply was clipped. 'I can manage.'

Petra pulled a face behind his back. Amos could be sensitive if he thought he was being fussed over, and he hated being reminded that he wasn't as young as he once was. The angina didn't help either, and Petra was always conscious that he might have an attack at any time. Besides, she was smaller than him, so it was easier to lever herself through the little square hatch.

She held her tongue though, not wanting to make him cross, and waited at the bottom of the ladder, listening to him clumping around up there and grizzling to himself.

Eventually he found what he was looking for, because he shouted, 'Watch out below!' and flung a box down through the hatch, nearly landing on Petra's head.

'Careful,' she cried as she dodged to the side.

'Sorry.'

He didn't sound sorry at all, and she narrowed her eyes. He'd done that on purpose.

While he slowly climbed down the ladder, Petra eyed the box, wondering what was in it.

She found out when he said, 'Go on then, what are you waiting for? Open it.'

Intrigued, Petra waited for him to reach the bottom of the ladder safely, then she bent down, picked up the box and walked into Amory's bedroom with it. Thankfully her son was still gurgling away, his eyes on the mobile which was gradually winding down. Hastily she wound it back up again, hoping for a few more minutes during which she could find out what was so important to make Amos decide to go up the attic at this very moment. Surely whatever it was could have waited? She was taking a hack out in an hour, and she had things to do.

She put the box on Amory's changing table and eased the lid off. Inside, underneath a layer of tissue paper, lay a mass of ivory lace.

Gently she lifted it out and gazed at the dress she was holding. 'Is this what I think it is?'

Amos grinned at her and nodded. 'Yep, your Aunt Mags wore it on her wedding day.'

Petra shot him an incredulous look. 'Do you honestly think I'm going to fit into this?' she asked. And it wasn't only the fit she was worried about – it looked so delicate she thought it might fall apart if she so much as sneezed.

'You won't know until you try it, will you?' Amos said. 'It might look tiny, but your Aunt Mags wasn't as slim as you.'

Petra studied it. Maybe her uncle was right. But even if he was, she wasn't sure she wanted to risk wearing it. 'It's beautiful, but—'

'I know what you're going to say.' Amos wagged his finger at her. 'I don't want any of that nonsense about it being too precious to wear. I'd prefer to see it get some action, rather than have it sit and rot in the attic, and I know your Aunt Mags would agree with me if she were alive.'

Petra still wasn't sure. She was honoured that he trusted her to wear it, but was it **her**? Compared to most of the other dresses she'd seen yesterday, it was quite old fashioned, almost Edwardian with its high neck and long sleeves. It was floor length, probably a little too long for her, but she could see that the length wouldn't matter as it would simply puddle around her feet. The lacy high neck was offset by long lace cuffs from mid-arm to wrists, and the same lace was repeated in the bodice. It had quite a wide band around the waist and flared out gently in a myriad of pleats and folds which cascaded to the floor, and the skirt of the dress had more lacework around the bottom. It was probably the most beautiful dress she'd ever seen, and something sparked inside her.

'Try it on,' Amos urged.

His eyes were suspiciously damp and she realised how emotional this was for him. Not only had he given Harry his wife's engagement ring for Harry to propose to her, which now sat on the third finger of her left hand, but he wanted her to wear Aunt Mag's wedding dress. The old photos didn't do it justice, because it was so much more beautiful in real life. She was surprised he still had it, but then again if she owned something this beautiful she wouldn't want to give it away or sell it either.

Petra left Amos with the baby, and took the dress into her bedroom. She was hesitant to try it. What if it didn't look right on her, or she didn't like it once it was on? It would be no good lying to him and saying it didn't fit because he'd expect to see her in it, so how could she tell him that she didn't want to wear it because she didn't think it suited her?

She slipped it over her head and wriggled her way into it. Then she looked in the mirror.

Oh, my!

Petra turned to one side then the other, examining herself from all angles. She wished it was full length, so she could see all of the dress, as she couldn't stand back far enough to be able to get it all in. But even from the bits she could see, she knew this was it. This was the dress. She hadn't managed to do it up by herself and she prayed that it would fit, because now that she'd seen it and tried it on, she couldn't imagine wearing anything else. If she couldn't do this up, then she'd go to her wedding wearing white jodhpurs and those white Wellington boots that she'd seen online with the ribbons on the side.

'Amos?' she called. 'Can you come in?'

Amos poked his head around the door and gasped, and when he stepped inside, tears were rolling down his face. 'You look...' He couldn't continue and hitched in an unsteady breath.

She turned and presented her back to him. 'Could you do me up? But don't force it: I don't want to risk tearing anything.'

She could feel his fingers trembling as he struggled to push the tiny seed-pearl buttons through the fabric loops, but eventually he got there and Petra was able to take a breath. She'd been trying to suck in her stomach and everything else, and had been scared to even breathe in case she ripped something.

'Turn around,' he said, his voice hoarse, and Petra turned slowly to face him.

Niece and uncle regarded each other solemnly.

'Well?' he said after a few moments, when he'd managed to compose himself.

'Thank you.' Petra was tongue-tied. She didn't have the words to describe how she was feeling – honoured, overwhelmed, beautiful. She never would have guessed that an item of clothing could make her feel as special as she did right now, and she couldn't wait to see Harry's face when she walked down the aisle of Picklewick's little church wearing it. She hoped he'd be impressed.

'I think we'd better sort a car out,' she said, unable to take her eyes off her reflection. 'I did think me and you could go to the church in the Land Rover, and the bridesmaids could meet us there, but now...'

'Over my dead body!' Amos exclaimed. 'If you think I'm going to let you travel to your wedding in a dirty old Land Rover, you can think again. I've already sorted out alternative transport.'

'What alternative transport?'

'Don't you worry your head about it,' he said. 'It's all in hand, and it will most definitely be better than the Land Rover.'

'I hope you haven't wasted money on a wedding car?' Petra said. What with all the money they'd invested in the cottages – which hadn't started bringing in any income yet – they couldn't afford fripperies like expensive wedding cars. When Petra had said she thought she'd better sort a car out, she'd been thinking of asking Luca to drive her and Amos to the church in his Range Rover.

'I haven't,' Amos assured her, and she heaved a sigh of relief at having yet another expense spared. She could also return the dress she'd bought to the department store, so that was an added bonus.

'I'd better take this off,' she said, on hearing an indignant squawk from her son. 'Can you keep it in your room? I don't want Harry to see it – I want it to be a surprise. I hope he'll like it.'

'He'll love it. I loved it when I saw Mags wearing it. I was standing in the front pew when the Wedding March started playing – in the same place that Harry will be waiting for you to walk down the aisle – and I turned around, and there she was. I had never seen anything so lovely in my life, and Harry will look at you and think the same.' He paused and Petra could see he wanted to say something else but was hesitating.

'What is it?' she asked.

'Are you sure about me walking you down the aisle? It should be your dad.'

'Amos, we've talked about this. Dad doesn't mind, honestly. You're like a father to me, and after all you've done for me—'

Amos leapt in. 'That's not the point,' he said, as she offered him her back so he could undo the buttons. His hands were more sure this time, although he continued to be very careful. 'Your father is still your father.'

'I know, and I do feel awful, but I am closer to you than I am to him.'

'That's sad,' he said. 'You only have one father—'

It was Petra's turn to interrupt. 'Not true,' she said. 'I've got my dad and I've got you.'

'How would you feel if...?' Amos cleared his throat before he carried on speaking. 'If both me and your dad walked you down the aisle? Would that be silly?'

Petra could have kissed him! 'What a brilliant solution,' she said. 'I should have thought of that.'

Amos chuckled.' You haven't really been thinking about the wedding at all, have you?'

'Is it that obvious?'

'Um...yeah?'

'Oh, dear. I hope Harry doesn't think that it's because I don't want to marry him, because I do, very much. I can't wait to be his wife.'

'He knows that – he knows what you're like. But now that the cottages are finished, you can spend next two weeks concentrating on your forthcoming nuptials.'

'I don't think there's a lot of concentrating left to be done,' Petra said. She'd got her dress and the bridesmaids had theirs, Amos was sorting out a car, the church had been booked, and her parents would be arriving on the Friday, and she was going to put them up in one of the cottages. Everyone knew she was getting married, so there was an open invitation for them to attend the church if they wanted. Not that she expected many people to turn up, and she was anticipating a small ceremony, but one thing she hadn't considered, which she supposed she should do, was the reception.

Amos was adamant that there was going to be some kind of celebration, but she didn't know what he was planning. Anyway, she decided to leave it up to him – he knew that she didn't want a big fuss, and if he decided to put on a bit of a buffet and invite a few people round for a glass of champagne, she wasn't going to object.

'It's a figure of speech,' Amos said. 'Anyway, everything is in hand, so there's no need for you to worry.'

Petra wasn't worried in the slightest. The only thing that mattered was that the church was booked, and that she and Harry turned up on time and said their vows. Anything else was window dressing. Anyway, aside from the church burning down or the vicar having a bout of dysentery, there wasn't much that could go wrong.

It was a beautiful day for a fete, Stephen thought, as he peered out of the living room window. The sky was brilliant blue and there wasn't a cloud in it, and when he opened the patio door and stepped outside he discovered it was already quite warm.

He inserted one of those little pods into the coffee machine and pressed the button, then leaned against the work top while he waited for it to brew. He knew that Julia was awake because he could hear the water running in her room and guessed she was in the shower.

Reflecting on yesterday he decided that all-in-all it had been a pretty good day. They'd managed to come to an understanding of sorts, despite one or two awkward moments, the first being when they'd discussed getting a divorce. There was still no resolution on that problem, but he didn't feel they needed to hurry. Neither of them wanted to move on when it came to their love lives, and they'd already sorted out and separated their finances, so there wasn't much else to do apart from sign on the dotted line. He knew it was the sensible thing to do to formalise their separation, but he just couldn't bring himself to do it. It seemed so final somehow, so he decided that unless Julie wanted to start divorce proceedings, he'd leave well alone for the time being. If he met someone else (ha! that was very unlikely) he'd revisit the subject and make a decision then.

The other really awkward moment had been when he'd said he would join her in the shower. He hadn't meant it like that, and he knew that Julie hadn't taken it like that, but for a split second the thought of his wife with water cascading over her shoulders, her hair wet, and her smooth skin fragrant from the shower gel she used, had made him feel weak with longing. Right at that very moment if she'd had said, 'Yes, join me,' he would have done. He had no doubt about that.

But he'd stumbled out an apology, and she'd stumbled out an acceptance, and they'd both hurried off to their respective bedrooms, Julie probably thinking what an idiot he was for even thinking that she might take it the wrong way, and Stephen feeling a right prat.

After that, the rest of the evening had been a bit like walking on eggshells, with Stephen very conscious of thinking before he spoke, in case he said the wrong thing again. He'd also been excruciatingly aware of her, of the expressions flitting across her face, of the sound of her voice, the way she delicately crossed her legs at the ankle, her smile...

He was reminded of when they'd first got together and he hadn't been able to take his eyes off her, soaking in every look, every curve, every expression, to savour during those times when they were apart.

How quickly had the awareness fled. He guessed all marriages were the same, familiarity wearing away at it like water eroding rock. He supposed they'd both taken each other for granted. It was one of the reasons he'd been looking forward to retiring, so they could reconnect as a couple without the distractions of work. He'd been thinking about telling her that he'd like them to travel, to discover new places together.

He snorted. He certainly didn't feel like travelling anymore. The idea didn't appeal to him at all now that he would be doing it alone.

'Can I smell coffee?' Julie asked, coming into the kitchen.

It was just about ready, so he handed her a cup, careful not to touch her. She was looking less ethereal this morning, her skin having absorbed some sun yesterday, which had given her more colour. She was still too thin, but she no longer looked as though she would shatter. It probably helped that she'd eaten better yesterday too: the exercise must have given her an appetite, because she'd polished off all of her portion of the picnic and she'd cleared her plate at dinner, which he was pleased to see.

She lifted the cup to her lips and closed her eyes briefly. 'Mmm, the first cup of coffee in the morning is always special,' she said, adding, 'Thank you. What time do you think we should leave?'

'I reckon a gentle stroll will take about half an hour, so what if we leave in an hour's time?'

'Perfect,' she said.

'Shall I do us some breakfast?'

'That would be lovely.'

As he pottered around in the kitchen, it almost felt like the last few months hadn't happened. If he ignored the ache in his chest, he could almost believe that they were still together and that they were enjoying a lovely weekend away.

Actually, he realised he **was** enjoying it. He'd enjoyed himself yesterday more than he'd enjoyed himself in a while. Since she'd told him she had been unfaithful, in fact.

The insight was a worry. Would he only ever be happy again if Julie was by his side? He guessed that he was also going through a form of mourning, and he was stricken with grief over the death of their marriage, but what if he never emerged from it? What if he was destined to spend the rest of his life yearning for Julie, but never allowing himself to forgive her?

He'd end up a lonely, miserable old git, that's what – and the thought wasn't a pleasant one.

Yesterday had brought what he was missing into sharp focus and now he didn't know what to do for the best.

'Toast and marmalade?' he suggested, pushing his troubled thoughts to the back of his mind and concentrating on getting some food inside her.

'Brilliant,' she said.

She smiled but it didn't reach her eyes and he hurriedly looked away. Sadness surrounded her like breath on a freezing day, and he wished he could do something to alleviate it. Not only did he dislike seeing her so unhappy, but her melancholy also served as a constant reminder and if he was honest he was sick of thinking about it. He wanted to forget it had ever happened. And today he intended to pretend that it hadn't; he wanted them to be a normal couple, doing normal things, despite knowing that he might be setting himself up for even more heartbreak.

The pain would be worth it.

CHAPTER SIX

'Oh, my word, I haven't seen a helter skelter in years!' Julie cried. 'Fancy a go?' She didn't mean it – she just wanted to see Stephen's face, and she burst out laughing at his horrified expression. 'No? How about the big wheel instead?' She widened her eyes hopefully.

'Not a chance. And neither am I going on the teacups, the dodgems or the pirate ship.'

'Spoilsport.'

'Tell you what, how about I find a bench to sit on and you can have a go?'

'Erm, that's okay,' she said.

'Chicken.'

Julie made clucking noises, earning herself an indulgent smile from a woman pushing a pram.

'People are staring.' Stephen nudged her, but he was grinning as he said it.

The contact was only fleeting, but she bit her lip at the surge of emotion it generated in her.

He edged away a little and a wash of colour spread up his neck, and she wondered whether he'd felt it too. She'd noticed that he'd been studiously avoiding touching her, and she guessed he must still be disgusted with her. He'd told her as much that awful day when she'd broken down and confessed her adultery. She would never forget the pain on his face, or the things he'd said to her. The worst thing he'd said was that he'd told her he still loved her. Then he'd walked out.

Pushing the memories away, she said, 'How about some lunch instead?'

'Good idea. Do you want to find a table in one of the cafes? Or the pub? Isaac said that the Black Horse does decent food.'

'Shall we save that for later? If you want to, that is.'

'Are you suggesting we go there for dinner tonight? It's a long trek to the cottage and back,' he warned.

'I thought we could stay in Picklewick for a few more hours, then have an early supper. Even if we don't leave until eight it should still be light enough to walk back, and if it isn't, we can get a taxi.'

'It's a plan,' he agreed.

It wasn't that Julie wanted to linger around the fair or watch the dog agility display which was on in an hour or so. Neither did she want to admire any woodcarving skills, or see which sheep won best of breed. Not going back to the cottage for several hours meant that Stephen's presence was diluted by the crowds of people, the noise, the activity. Being in such close proximity to him was difficult enough, without it being on a one-to-one basis. And if they stayed in the village until early evening, it might be late enough by the time they got back to the cottage to just have a quick nightcap and then slope off to bed, where she could weep in peace.

She really did feel like crying, but her tears were no longer for Emrys. They were for her and Stephen, and for what she'd destroyed. If only she had been able to hold herself together, she could have grieved for Emrys in private and Stephen would have been none the wiser. What good had knowing done him?

With a bright smile she nodded towards a group of pop-up eateries. 'Fancy taking a look at those?'

The smells drifting in the warm late-summer air were mouth-watering and Julie was surprised to discover she had an appetite. She'd gone from pushing Amos's casserole around on her plate on Friday evening, to scoffing everything put in front of her yesterday.

She assumed it was because of the unaccustomed exercise. After hardly leaving the house for months, apart from a few necessary visits to the shops, she'd gone for two long walks in the countryside in as many days. Three, if she counted the walk into Picklewick earlier today. When she returned home she decided it might be a good idea to incorporate a walk into her daily routine. But even as she considered it, she knew she wouldn't – going for a walk on her own didn't appeal in the slightest.

They came to a halt at the first of the food vans, which was selling pulled pork baguettes made from wild boar with caramelised onions and a quince chutney, and Julie inhaled the delicious aroma.

'Want one?' Stephen asked.

'I don't think I can manage a whole one,' she said. Despite her new-found appetite, the baguettes were the length of her forearm.

'We could share, and if we're still hungry we could try something else afterwards?' he suggested.

A lump came to Julie's throat. They used to do the very same thing whenever they went out, even if they only popped into a cafe for coffee and cake. She'd choose one thing and he'd choose another, and they would share.

Not trusting herself to speak, all she could do was nod.

Stephen ordered and bought a couple of chilled cans of lemonade to go with their food, and they strolled around the fete nibbling at their lunch and taking it all in.

'Look, there's Amos,' Julie said, spotting him talking to a woman of roughly the same age. He had Petra's baby with him, and looked every inch the proud grandad.

Amos waved when he saw them and Julie made her way over to him, Stephen following.

She cooed at the little boy and stroked his downy cheek, and the baby grinned back at her, his smile dribbly and gummy.

'How are you enjoying it so far?' Amos asked, before remembering to introduce himself to Stephen. 'Sorry, I'm Amos, and this is Lena. A friend.'

Something about the way he said the word **friend** made Julie wonder if there was more than friendship going on.

Amos lowered his voice and glanced around. 'She's helping with the wedding arrangements, but don't tell Petra. She's got no idea we're having a big reception in the arena at the stables. It's all hush hush.'

'How lovely! It's not long now, is it?' Julie said, taking both Amos and Lena in with a smile.

'Thirteen days. And there's still so much to do.'

'Anything we can help with?' Julie said 'we' without thinking, and she glanced at Stephen apologetically. However, he was nodding, so she assumed he wasn't put out at being included in the offer.

'It's all in hand,' Amos said, 'but thank you anyway. The hardest part will be keeping Petra away from the arena and the stables on the morning, because that's when we'll be setting it up and decorating it. She's going to want to do her usual morning routine of checking on the horses.'

'But it's her wedding day!' Julie said.

'You don't know Petra,' Lena replied grimly. 'She lives and breathes horses. My daughter, October, is the same. She works at the stables, and between us we're trying to hatch a plan to get Petra away from the place for the night, but I don't think we'll be able to manage it.'

'Could you book her into a hotel somewhere?' Julie wondered.

Amos pulled a face. 'Not really; the only place in Picklewick is the Black Horse, and she's not going to see the point in staying there when she has a perfectly good bedroom at the stables. Then there's Amory to consider – he'll be better off at home on the night before the wedding, because Petra will have enough on her plate without worrying whether she remembered to pack the nappy cream.'

All four adults looked at the baby, who gazed serenely back at them.

'Oh, dear. I'm sure you'll work something out,' Julie said.

'I hope so.'

'Good luck,' Julie said, giving the baby another huge smile. Amory beamed back. 'Remember when Isaac was that age?' she asked Stephen as they walked away. 'He wasn't as happy as that little chap.'

'He was a bit of a misery, wasn't he?' Stephen agreed. 'He didn't stop crying for at least six months. I kept wondering what we were doing wrong!'

'He's turned out okay though, hasn't he?'

'He's more than okay. He's a credit to us, even if I do say so myself.'

'Do you think he and Nelly will get married?'

'I wouldn't be surprised. He's absolutely besotted with her.'

'And she him,' Julie said. 'A right pair of love birds, they are. It makes my heart melt just seeing them.'

'We used to—' Stephen stopped abruptly.

'Yes, we did.' She could see him looking at her out of the corner of his eye, and she guessed he was wondering whether it had all been an act on her part.

It hadn't. She had genuinely loved her husband. She still did.

But she had loved Emrys more.

For a while.

It had taken losing Stephen for her to realise that for all those years the love she'd had for her husband had grown and deepened, until he'd eventually become as necessary to her as the very air she breathed.

Emrys was her past, her youth, and her first love: Stephen had been her present, her future, and her enduring love.

Until she'd driven him away.

Three glasses of wine at dinner had gone to Julie's head, Stephen thought. To be fair, he'd had a pint before their meal at the Black Horse and he'd also had two glasses of wine with it, so he was faring only marginally better than she. They should have been sensible and called for a taxi to take them back to the cottage, but it was such a lovely evening that they'd decided to walk.

Stephen was starting to regret it now, because Julie wasn't as steady on her feet as him, and every so often he was forced to catch hold of her as she stumbled up the rough path leading from Picklewick to the stables. Going up the hill was harder than going down and was taking longer too, so the estimated half hour walk back was turning into an hour. And having to hold her hand as she picked her way up the path was excruciating.

Still, he'd enjoyed the day at the fete and he'd enjoyed the meal. He'd also enjoyed Julie's company – far more than he'd have thought possible prior to this weekend, and far more than was wise, considering the situation.

Gosh, he'd missed her so much, and he hadn't fully realised just how deeply until now. The thought of going back to his lonely rented house tomorrow filled him with dread.

As he put an arm around his wife's waist to steady her, he wondered how she felt about living alone in the house they'd shared for over thirty years. Was she as lonely as him, or was she glad she had the freedom to mourn Emrys without his disapproving presence?

His fingers tingled where he held her, and when she leant into him for support his heart gave a lurch. He'd been feeling this way since they'd left the pub – his heart thudding, his mouth dry, and he had been fighting an overwhelming longing to gather her to him and kiss her until she begged him to stop.

'Not far to go now,' he said, as they crested a small rise.

It was still light – just – and he could make out the stables in the deepening gloom, relieved to find that another ten minutes or so should bring them to the door of their cottage.

Knee-high grass lay to either side of the narrow path that they were trekking along and wavelike ripples danced across its golden surface. The sky held a fast-fading reminder of the day in the swathe of russet colours where the sun had dipped below the horizon, a harbinger of approaching autumn.

They were now walking in single file so as not to trample the grass, and when Julie came to a sudden halt, he bumped into her.

'Sorry,' he mumbled, a waft of her familiar perfume assaulting his nostrils once again.

'Look,' she breathed, her eyes scanning the valley. 'Isn't it beautiful?'

It was, but he didn't mean the view. He was gazing at his wife. Her face was serene, a gentle smile playing about her mouth. Her eyes shone in the gloaming, and the fading day lit her in soft focus.

'I'm glad you stayed,' she said. 'Being here wouldn't have been the same on my own.'

'It's been a good couple of days,' he agreed, his voice hoarse, and he cleared his throat.

'I'd say we should do this more often, but...' she tailed off sadly.

He wanted to suggest that they make this an annual thing, but he couldn't bring himself to contemplate another whole year without her. The bleakness of it sent shivers of despair through his very soul. He didn't want to think of getting to the end of another 365 days, and nothing having changed in his life. Something would have to give, but he didn't know what. What he did know was that he couldn't face another twelve months of his life the way it was.

As though she sensed his dark thoughts, Julie shivered.

He said, 'Come on, let's get inside. You're cold.'

'I'm fine; someone's just walked over my grave, that's all.'

Stephen gave her a sharp look. She had sensed his mood, and it sent a tremor down his own spine. He and Julie used to be so in-tune with one another that it was almost as though they'd read each other's minds. It appeared the connection was still there.

In a sudden burst of anger, he grunted at his stupidity. If he really had been so in-tune with his wife, surely he would have realised that she'd loved someone else for all these years?

Then he let out a slow breath and drove it away. Anger was such a fruitless and negative emotion, and holding on to it did no one any good. He supposed that intense emotions like the ones he'd been feeling since that fateful day last November were unlikely to disappear overnight, and he realised that the heartbreak probably wouldn't fully leave him, although he hoped it would fade with time.

'Here we are,' he said, sounding unnecessarily cheerful as they approached the cottage. He fished the keys out of his pocket and unlocked the door, pushing it open to allow her to step inside ahead of him.

She hesitated for a second, then went in.

He followed more slowly. He hadn't missed the tears in her eyes, and her sadness pricked him to the core.

'Drink?' she asked, her back to him.

She'd paused in the kitchen doorway, her shoulders up around her ears, her back rigid. He fought the urge to massage the tension away with his strong hands.

'Gin?' he suggested. 'You brought enough with you.' His tone was deliberately light as he tried to alleviate the tension.

He left her to it and went to stand by the patio doors. The garden was in darkness and his reflection stared back at him. The face gazing out belonged to a stranger. Where had all the years gone? When had he become this middle-aged man?

He closed his eyes, a flashback of Julie on their wedding night swooping through his mind and catching him unawares.

They had spent it in an airport hotel because they were flying to Paris for their honeymoon the following day. He'd been in the bathroom, having just cleaned his teeth, feeling unaccountably nervous even though he wasn't a stranger to her body. He knew it as well as he knew his own, but tonight – the first time they would make love as a married couple – held a deep significance for him.

Julie had come in behind him and he'd seen her reflection in the glass above the basin. She'd been naked...

He watched her approach now, a tumbler in each hand, a ghostly figure in the glass, and he pushed the memories away.

Thinking those kinds of thoughts wouldn't do any good at all.

'Thanks.' He sipped at his drink, and their eyes met in the glass of the door.

She held his gaze, hers unwavering, and slowly, oh so slowly, he turned to face her.

Just as slowly he took her drink from her and placed both tumblers on the table, his eyes never leaving hers.

He couldn't say why he did it, why he kissed her. He just did.

And it felt like coming home.

CHAPTER SEVEN

Without opening her eyes, Julie knew that she was on her own in the bed, but just to make sure she opened them anyway and her hand slid across to the side Stephen usually slept on. The duvet was pushed back and there was a dent in the pillow where his head had rested. The sheet was cold. He hadn't just left; he'd been gone a while.

However, she could hear the shower in the other bedroom running, and she smiled to herself. He always did have a tendency to wake up earlier than her, and he would often sneak out of bed and go downstairs, ready to start his day long before she emerged from the land of Nod. She wondered how long he'd been up, and when she glanced at the clock she saw that it was already nine. She hadn't slept this well in a very long time, and her insides tingled as she thought of the reason why.

When Isaac had asked her if she'd like to spend a weekend in a cottage as a favour to him, the last thing she'd imagined was that Stephen would also be there. Even when she'd come back from the house up at the stables, clutching that casserole in her hands, and had spotted her estranged husband in the kitchen peering into the fridge, not in a million years did she think that they might end up in bed together.

But they had, and it had been wonderful.

Aside from them getting back together, for which she was profoundly thankful and grateful, the sex had been amazing. Like most couples, they'd had make-up sex after an argument, but it had been nothing like last night. She had felt such a profound connexion to him, that it touched her soul.

Her heart was still singing this morning and a deep contentment spread through her bones, making her feel languid and satiated, and she would be quite happy to stay in bed for the rest of the day – as long as Stephen was under the covers with her, of course.

She'd get up in a few minutes, have a shower, and then she'd entice him back to bed. She wasn't entirely sure what time Isaac was coming – she thought he'd mentioned something about eleven o'clock, but that was two hours away. A great deal could happen in two hours.

Briefly she wondered why Stephen hadn't used the shower in her room, but then she realised how thoughtful he was being. The shower would have woken her up, and he'd probably wanted to let her sleep. Aw, how sweet. Also, it made sense for him to use that one, considering all his clothes were in the other bedroom. She wondered whether he would bother getting dressed, or whether he'd pad into her bedroom, naked and expectant, so they could continue where they'd left off last night.

The thought made her toes curl with delicious anticipation. He'd been tender at first, hesitant almost, then passion had taken over and she bit her lip at the memory. He'd been almost animalistic, focused and driven, yet her passion had matched his. She could still feel his hands on her body, here his groans of delight, feel his—

Whoa, girlie, she said to herself, recognising that she could probably do with a shower herself before she leapt on him again. She'd also like some tea. And maybe some breakfast. All that physical activity yesterday (she nearly giggled when she thought of precisely what that physical activity had entailed) had given her an appetite. As soon as her hunger for food was satisfied, she could think about satisfying a hunger of an entirely different kind.

Julie could feel the grin on her face, and she let out a little squeak of happiness. After nine long months and all the despair and heartache, she and Stephen were back together. And she had finally exercised Emrys's ghost. She'd always have a special place in her heart for her first true love, but he no longer dominated it. Stephen had that honour and had done for a long time, had she been aware of it. It had taken the news of Emrys's death for her to fully appreciate how deep her love for Stephen was, and how right they were together. He brought out the best in her and complemented her perfectly. They were different sides of the same coin, neither of them complete without the other.

She pushed the duvet back and sat up. The shower in the other room was still going, so she decided to nip downstairs to put the kettle on and prepare some breakfast, so when Stephen came down she could simply put it in front of him. She thought about putting something else in front of him too, the innuendo making her giggle, but she'd wait until after they'd eaten.

Sliding her feet into her slippers, she put on the little wrap that was draped over a chair in the corner. There was no need to get dressed because she intended to get naked again very soon and the wrap would cover her modesty for the time being.

Scrambled eggs, that's what she fancied. Fluffy yellow egginess on hot buttered toast. Mmm...her mouth watered, and she realised her appetite had returned with a vengeance. It had been creeping back over the course of the weekend, and now she could feel hunger pangs clawing at her stomach despite the amount she ate yesterday. The meal in the Black Horse had been delicious, and she'd polished off every morsel on her plate and had even eaten pudding.

She found she was looking forward to getting back into the kitchen again and cooking proper meals for her and Stephen. The only time she'd really bothered cooking since he'd left had been when Isaac came for lunch or dinner, but she only cooked to stop their son from worrying about her.

Well, there was no need for him to worry anymore, was there. She was aware that she'd lost weight over the past few months, and she was also aware how quickly she would put it all back on again once she started eating more regularly.

She would have to keep an eye on that. She quite liked the new slender her, although she didn't care much for the reason for the weight loss. She could afford to put on a few pounds, but not too many. Anyway, she'd probably get far more exercise when Stephen moved back in, she guessed, giggling to herself once more.

She couldn't wait. In fact, when Isaac returned with Stephen's car keys, she would tell him that there was no need for him to take her home. Stephen could do it. They could call around to the place he was renting on their way, and pick up a few things for his immediate needs, just to see him through the next few days. There was no rush for him to move everything out and back into the marital home, although she would prefer him to do it sooner rather than later. No doubt he'd have to give a month's notice on his lease, so that would give him plenty of time to clear out the place and decide what, if anything, he wanted to keep.

Of course, she had never set foot in it, although Isaac had, and he'd told her it was quite basic, so she couldn't imagine Stephen would want to bring much with him. She certainly didn't expect him to bring big things like his bed or sofa. If his landlord was willing, Stephen could leave those items there for the next person who moved in, or if that wasn't appropriate, he could arrange for someone from one of the local charities to pick up any large items he didn't want.

She got the eggs out of the fridge and cracked them one by one into a bowl, then whisked them up with a little salt and pepper and a tiny drop of milk. As she worked, she realised she was humming, and it made her smile. It had been a long time since she'd hummed, and a flame of pure happiness ignited in her chest. Last November she thought she'd never be happy again, but how wrong could she be. She was almost delirious with it right now, excitement flitting through her as she planned for their future.

Ever since he'd walked out, Julie had barely thought more than a day ahead. But now she was thinking that perhaps they could go on holiday at half term. Somewhere hot and exotic. Somewhere where they could be waited on and spoilt, and spend hours floating in the sea and kissing. She'd never kissed in the sea before and she quite fancied trying it.

A morning spent at the beach, a leisurely lunch, then an afternoon siesta, which she hoped would consist of very little sleeping, sounded idyllic. Okay, maybe a nap afterwards, because they weren't getting any younger.

Another giggle escaped her, lighthearted and girly.

She was so happy, she could cry.

The water trickling down Stephen's face wasn't just from the shower. He was leaning against the tiles, his eyes burning, his chest heaving with silent sobs, crying so hard it hurt.

What had he done?

How could he have been so stupid?

He'd made a complete hash of this weekend. Why, oh why, had he thought he could spend three days with Julie and not suffer the consequences?

Last night he'd given in to his loneliness, given into his love and his desire for her, and he'd ended up in her bed. It might have been indescribably perfect, but that didn't stop him from regretting what he'd done.

Even as he'd been making love to her, a little voice in his head had been telling him to stop, that he'd regret it, that it wasn't a good idea; but he'd ignored it. He hadn't been able to stop. He'd wanted her so badly, and from the way she clutched at him, the way her nails had scratched his back, and her soft whimpers of pleasure, she had wanted it as much as he. He'd so completely lost himself in the taste of her, in the feel of her skin, and her passion, that common sense had deserted him.

Why hadn't he listened to it? In ignoring it, he'd succeeded in heaping misery on top of heartache, because although he might have made peace with himself when it came to his feelings of betrayal over what she'd done, he could never forget.

He must have been out of his mind. There was no way they could go back to the way they were. And now he'd made things a hundred times worse.

He couldn't face the future without her, but neither did he feel able to let her back into his life and risk yet more pain. He didn't think he could cope with it. He'd been barely coping as it was.

Lifting his head, he let the water sluice down his cheeks to wash away the scalding tears. He couldn't let her see him like this, so he heaved in one final hitching breath and let it out slowly. He was done crying for now, although he guessed he'd do more of it before the day was out. As soon as Isaac appeared with his keys, he'd leave. He'd go back to his rented house, lock the door and wallow in misery. And he'd probably carry on wallowing until a week Thursday when the new term started and he'd have no choice other than to go to work and pretend everything was normal.

To be honest, he didn't want to go back to his sad, lonely house, and neither did he feel he could face his job. In fact, he didn't want to carry on living the life he'd been living for the past few months, but what else could he do?

Turning the shower off, he reached for the towel hanging on the rail outside the cubicle and wiped his face.

Suddenly he stopped towelling himself dry as a thought struck him.

He'd go travelling, that's what he'd do.

He'd let the school know he was taking early retirement and ask how soon they'd be able to release him. If he was lucky, he might be on the other side of the world by October half term.

The plan didn't fill him with as much excitement as it should have done. It didn't fill him with any excitement at all, but it was better than moping around, day in, day out. At least he wouldn't run the risk of bumping into Julie in a supermarket – or give Isaac another opportunity to set them up again.

With a heavy heart, Stephen finished drying himself off and pulled on some clothes, hastily stuffing everything else into his holdall so he'd be ready to leave as soon as Isaac showed up.

After a final look around to make sure he hadn't forgotten to pack anything, he made his way downstairs. He couldn't put it off seeing Julie any longer. He knew she was awake because he could hear her in the kitchen, and he wondered if she was also feeling bad about last night. No doubt she was regretting it as much as he. How could she not when she was in love with someone else? She might be married to him, but it was Emrys she really loved, Emrys who she'd been breaking her heart over.

These past few days it had been so easy to slip back into their old ways and the familiar lovemaking, that it must have taken her as much by surprise as it had him. He hoped she wasn't beating herself up over it, like he was, but he suspected she probably would be.

With these thoughts in his mind and fully expecting to find Julie in as much distress as he over the events of the previous night, he was shocked to see her cooking scrambled eggs, her body moving gently from side to side as she chased the mixture around the pan to ensure it was thoroughly cooked. Not only that, but she was **humming**.

He swallowed, dread spearing him in the stomach. Oh, god, she **wasn't** regretting it. She was happy about it. And when she glanced up from the stove and saw him standing there, her smile tore his heart in two. She looked radiant, and more beautiful than he had ever seen her look before.

'I'm making us some scrambled eggs,' she said. 'The toast is about to pop any second – can you butter it?'

'Julie...?'

'Oh, and there's tea in the pot if you want to pour yourself a cup.'

'Julie.'

'What?' She stopped stirring the eggs and peered at them. 'I think these are just about done.'

'**Julie!** Please, just stop...We need to talk.'

The miserable expression on her face would stay with him for the rest of his life.

The sound of a car engine outside made Julie look out of the window, hoping it was Isaac coming to fetch her. She couldn't wait to get out of this place and away from Stephen. Since he'd informed her that last night had been a mistake and that he was sorry it had happened, she'd been hiding in her bedroom, watching the minutes tick slowly by and trying to stem the tears that flowed from her eyes in a steady stream.

 Her relief when she saw her son sauntering towards the row of cottages almost had her sobbing out loud.

Hastily, she dabbed a tissue under her red and swollen eyes, then blew her nose. She knew she looked a mess and that Stephen and Isaac would realise she had been crying but there was nothing she could do about that. In fact, it would serve them both right to see the hurt they'd caused.

Isaac's actions in throwing her and Stephen together for the weekend might have been coming from a good place, but he'd done more harm than good. And Stephen must be extremely pleased with himself for executing such a fitting revenge: he'd made love to her so expertly and thoroughly that his passion and tenderness had led her to believe they had a second chance at love.

How wrong could she be.

He must have been laughing his socks off when he'd seen her playing happy families in the kitchen, knowing that she was thinking that they were back together and that everything could return to the way it had been.

More fool her. She should have known Stephen wouldn't find it easy to forgive and forget what she'd done. Although he had never been a vindictive man and he'd never been one to hold a grudge, he'd made it clear when he'd left her all those months ago that they were over. Isaac throwing them together must have seemed an ideal opportunity for Stephen to get his own back.

She doubted whether he'd started out with that intention, because he'd probably thought she was still grieving for Emrys, but over the last two days when they had appeared to reconnect, he must have decided to love her and leave her.

Or, even worse, had she merely been an opportunity to get his leg over?

The thought made her want to cry again, just when she'd managed to stem the flow, and she hurriedly blew her nose again and cleared her throat, before splashing some cold water on her face and checking her appearance.

She didn't like what she saw in the mirror but that couldn't be helped, so she grabbed her jacket, her bag and her case, and trundled downstairs.

She had just got to the bottom of the stairs when she heard voices, and she hurried to the front door to find Isaac and his father outside. Stephen's bag rested on the bench below the window, and she assumed that he had been waiting in eager anticipation for Isaac to arrive.

'Why, what's happened?' she heard Isaac ask.

'Nothing. Can I have my keys, there is somewhere I need to be.' Stephen's voice was short and clipped.

Nothing? She'd hardly describe what had happened last night as **nothing.** But perhaps that is exactly how her husband thought of her.

Julie bit her lip, holding back a sob, and busied herself with putting on her jacket and slinging her bag over her arm, so that neither her husband nor her son could see how upset she was.

Isaac was looking at his dad with a bewildered expression. 'Did you have a good time?'

'It was all right.' Stephen was gruff. He held his hand out for the keys and Isaac pulled them out of his pocket and placed them in his palm.

Stephen's fingers curled around them and he nodded once. 'Right then, I'll be off.' He picked up his bag and began to walk away.

Isaac said, 'Have you got any recommendations for Petra?'

'I'll email them to you.' Stephen waved a hand in the air and kept on walking.

'At least say goodbye to Mum,' Isaac called after him.

Stephen faltered for a second before carrying on up the path, and Julie realised that was all the acknowledgement she was going to get.

'What's up with Dad?' Isaac turned to her.

'You'd better ask him.'

'Have you been crying? Mum? Is everything okay?'

'No, it's not.'

'What happened?'

'You tricked me and your father into spending the weekend together. What do you think happened?'

Isaac stared at her, his expression bleak. 'Did you have a fight?'

'Worse. We slept together.' Julie gleaned a small amount of satisfaction when she saw her son wince. 'What did you expect would happen?'

'Erm...I **hoped** you'd kiss and make up.'

'You got the kissing part right,' she said. 'But we haven't made up.' Suddenly angry at Isaac for putting her in this position, she rounded on him. 'What did you expect, eh? We're not a pair of little kids who've had a squabble over a crayon.'

'But you just said you'd...er...'

'We did. Look, Isaac, I don't want to talk about it. Your father has made it perfectly clear that he's not going to forgive me and I don't blame him. I'm not sure I could forgive me, either. In fact, I don't. So please don't ask any more questions. Just take me home.'

'Oh Mum, I'm so sorry.'

Julie nodded, not trusting herself to speak.

Without another word, he picked up her case and closed the door, and they drove home in silence, the only noise being Julie's quiet snuffles as she tried to contain her heartache.

CHAPTER EIGHT

Julie studied the photo on her phone and smiled sadly, although it wasn't the photo itself that made her sad, it was the memories it evoked.

Isaac did look handsome though, and Nelly was gorgeous in a light blue dress and high heels. Her hair was a loose cloud about her shoulders and the pair of them appeared to be very much in love.

They were on their way to Petra and Harry's wedding, and it was the event itself that brought Julie's memories of the weekend she'd spent at the cottage the other week flooding back. She had been trying not to think about it, but it hadn't been easy. And when it came to crying, the slightest thing set her off.

Tears pricked at her eyes now, and she brushed them away with an impatient swipe of her hand. She was starting to get on her own nerves, so goodness knows how irritating she must be to Isaac. Bless him, he didn't show it. He'd been full of remorse and contrition these past two weeks, and had been going out of his way to pop in and see her most days.

Julie realised she must have worried him a fair bit on the drive back from the stables on Muddypuddle Lane, because she'd sobbed steadily the whole time.

She didn't know whether he'd spoken to his father about what had happened, or how Stephen was feeling about it. Smug maybe? Justified? Or maybe he didn't feel anything at all and hadn't given her a second thought. The latter was the more likely scenario. And the most hurtful.

She, on the other hand, hadn't been able to stop thinking about it and wishing she hadn't agreed to spend the weekend in the cottage in the first place. Or hadn't agreed when Stephen had suggested that they give it a go together. If she'd had even the smallest inkling of how badly it would end, she'd have walked into Picklewick on that Friday evening and would have arranged for a taxi to take her home. But hindsight is a wonderful thing, and she had stayed to suffer the consequences instead.

She sent Isaac a quick message back, telling him how lovely they looked and telling them to have a good time, and afterwards she couldn't help wondering how Amos had got on with setting up the reception, and whether Petra had found out about it ahead of time. Which brought the image of her and Stephen chatting to

Amos at Picklewick's fete to mind. If only she hadn't suggested going to the Black Horse for a meal, she wouldn't have drunk three glasses of wine and she might have kept a tighter rein on her emotions.

Oh, well, what was done, was done. She couldn't change anything so there was no point in dwelling on it – but that was easier said than done, wasn't it?

'Keep still,' October urged, slapping Petra gently on the arm. 'I can't do these fiddly buttons up if you keep squirming around.'

Petra stopped fidgeting long enough for October to finish buttoning her into her wedding dress. She was already nervous but as the morning wore on she had been finding it increasingly difficult to sit still. Something was bothering her, but she didn't know what.

It wasn't anything to do with Harry because she'd spoken to him on the phone this morning. He'd spent the night at Timothy and Charity's cottage, and right at this moment she guessed he was going through the same process, although he'd be getting into a suit not a dress. Amos had picked some flowers from the garden and had dropped them down to Timothy's house, for buttonholes, so that wasn't what was niggling at her. And she knew Harry was planning on being at the church a good fifteen minutes before she was due to arrive, so that wasn't it, either. There was no car to worry about for him, because it was only a three-minute walk. And Luca was driving her, Amos and her dad to the church in his car.

Petra turned her attention to her son who was currently being entertained by Lena.

Knowing that Petra and Amos would be up to their eyes in it this morning, Lena had offered to pop up to the stables to look after Amory while they got ready.

Petra's mum and dad, who were staying in one of the cottages, had also offered, but Amory had only seen them once since he'd been born, and as far as he was concerned they were total strangers, so Petra hadn't taken them up on it. Amory knew Lena and liked her, and she was very good with him, so Petra was happy for her to take care of him this morning while she was getting ready. Then she guessed he'd be passed around like a parcel until the ceremony was over, and after that she would rescue him. He'd probably be ready for a feed by then, anyway.

In anticipation at not being able to get in and out of her dress very easily, Petra had expressed some milk, and for the past couple of weeks she had gradually introduced him to the bottle, which he had taken to with some reluctance, but at least he drank it.

Petra listened intently, but all she could hear was Lena playing peekaboo, and Amory's endearing little giggles, so she knew there wasn't an issue there.

She'd checked and double checked that his changing bag contained everything he could possibly need, and she knew Lena would leave it until the last moment before swapping his babygro for the little outfit that Harry had bought him especially for the occasion. If they dressed him in it too soon, it was guaranteed Amory would be sick all over it, or worse.

Amos was fine, too. He was already dressed in his suit, and he kept poking his head around her bedroom door to check on progress. He'd seemed quite flummoxed when on the first occasion, expecting to see Petra fully dressed, he had found her wearing a tatty old dressing gown. October had been standing behind her with a comb clamped in her teeth and her curling tongs in hand, and Charity had been crouching down in front of her, staring intently at Petra's face, and wielding a small brush. Megan had been in the middle of popping a cork on something alcoholic and bubbly, and Amos had taken one look at the four of them and had beaten a hasty retreat.

So what was it that was putting her on edge?

'You look stunning,' Megan said, handing Petra another glass of champagne.

Petra hadn't touched the first one yet. She wanted to keep a clear head, and anyway she was still feeding Amory, so alcohol was out of bounds.

Petra looked in the mirror for the first time since the three women had descended on her with the express intention of turning her from a horse rider into a bride, and she didn't recognise herself. Gone was the make-up-free face, the messy ponytail and jodhpur-wearing reflection she was used to seeing. In its place was a vision in ivory silk and lace, with subtle makeup and artfully styled hair.

She turned to her three bridesmaids in horror. 'Harry's not going to recognise me!' she cried.

October chuckled. 'I think he will. He's going to think you look beautiful.'

Petra looked in the mirror again, then glanced back at October. 'Do you think?'

'Definitely. Now, are you ready?'

'I don't know,' Petra said, feeling a sudden attack of unwelcome and unexpected nerves.

When she got to the church all those people would be looking at her, and the thought was terrifying. Few people had actually been invited to the wedding but she had a feeling that half of Picklewick might turn up, and the thought of all those eyes trained on her made her feel sick. Which was silly really, considering she was happy enough to be the centre of attention when she was in the arena, conducting classes, or ensuring a gymkhana went smoothly. But she knew what she was doing when it came to horses. She was entirely out of her comfort zone when it came to weddings.

'Are you going to tell me what you've been up to?' she demanded. Perhaps that's what the problem was? Maybe the fact that she hadn't been allowed anywhere near the stable block or the arena this morning was making her nervous. Bless them, October, Charity and Nathan had insisted on seeing to the horses, even though she had been itching to get outside and do what she always did.

Amos had backed them up. 'It's your wedding day,' he'd told her firmly. 'Just take it easy and relax. Spend some time with Amory and pamper yourself.'

Petra wasn't sure what pampering herself entailed. She wasn't a pampering herself sort of person. She might shave her legs and armpits, but that's about as far as it went. Oh, and she did slather moisturiser on her skin every evening after her shower, but that was because she was outside a lot and the wind and the sun tended to be drying on any exposed areas, so it was more a case of damage control rather than a beauty regime. And she had never used a face mask or a bath bomb in her life and she didn't intend to start now, wedding day or not.

Instead, she'd moped around, peering out of the window now and again, and wondering what was going on – because clearly something was. Although she wasn't a hundred per cent certain, she was convinced she'd heard more than the usual stable noises earlier, and everyone seemed furtive and anxious to keep her in the house. Which made her itch to go outside even more.

'Well?' she demanded, when it didn't seem she was going to get an answer. 'I'm not going anywhere until you tell me.'

Her maid-of-honour and the two bridesmaids shared a look. October shrugged and Charity nodded. Megan pulled a face.

'Okay,' Megan said. 'But you've got to act surprised and if anyone asks you didn't get it from us.'

'What?'

'Amos and Harry have arranged a reception and a party in the arena,' Megan said in a rush. 'Harry has been up half the night, and Timothy too, decorating it, laying out tables, arranging flowers. Amos and Nathan helped, and so did quite a few others.'

Petra was stunned. She hadn't been expecting that. She had been thinking that there was something wrong with one of the horses and they were keeping it from her so as not to worry her.

'I didn't want a fuss,' she objected.

Megan narrowed her eyes. 'Tough, you're having one. Oh, and your mum and dad helped as well. They've sorted out the food.'

'What food?'

'You can't have a wedding reception without food. It was delivered to the cottages earlier. While you and Harry are having your photos taken outside the church, William has arranged for some of his staff at the care home to come up to the stables and set it all out ready.'

Petra felt faint. 'Why?' was all she managed to squeak.

'Because you deserve a special day with everyone who loves you,' Megan said.

Petra was astonished to feel a prickle of tears in the back of her eyes, and she blinked furiously.

'Don't you dare cry,' Charity warned. 'You'll spoil your makeup.'

'I never cry,' Petra said, then promptly burst into tears, evoking a flurry of activity as her bridesmaid's attempted to limit the damage.

She'd been overwhelmed with gratitude at the number of people who had turned out to help clear the old cow shed before the builders arrived to do their part. But this was even more amazing, and she was overcome with emotion.

Suddenly she was delighted that she and Harry weren't having a small ceremony – she wanted to proclaim her love for him from the rooftops and she wanted everyone there when she did. She never realised so many people cared, and her heart constricted with love and gratitude.

'There's one more thing,' October said. 'If you're ready, come outside and see.'

'We've got to leave in a minute,' Petra warned, clocking the time. She needed to be at the church in half an hour. 'Is Luca here?'

'He's here – he's been here for a while, helping decorate the arena.' October grinned. 'Come on, you've got to see this!'

October's excitement was catching, and Petra allowed herself to be led down the stairs, Megan following closely behind to hold the skirt of Petra's dress off the floor.

'Close your eyes,' Charity instructed, nodding to Amos who was waiting in the hall. The front door was shut, but he didn't open it until Petra closed her eyes.

With October and Amos guiding her, Petra was tentatively led outside and brought to a halt on the step. She felt the sun on her face and was grateful that the weather had held. It hadn't rained for several weeks, but it would have been just her luck for it to pour down today.

The breeze blowing gently across her face held the heady perfume of the flowers which were growing around the door, the unmistakable aroma of horses, and a faint but sharp tang of smoke, and she wondered if Amos was planning to serve barbeque food at the reception later.

'Open your eyes!' Amos cried.

Petra took a deep breath and slowly opened them.

In front of her was a white open-topped carriage, with two horses standing between the shafts. Their coats gleamed in the sunlight and the harnesses twinkled and jingled as they tossed their heads.

'That's Storm and Midnight!' she exclaimed. 'How? When—?' She glanced at the people gathered around – Amos, Megan, October, Charity, Luca, Nathan, Lena, her parents – and she felt like crying again.

'You can blame October,' Amos said. 'It was her idea. Harry happened to mention seeing an old carriage when he was shoeing a horse a couple of months ago, and she thought it might be a good idea to train Storm and Midnight to pull it, to take you to the church. So he bought it, and has spent the last few weeks doing it up. What do you think?'

'It's gorgeous,' she said. So that's what he'd been up to. She gazed at it an awe. It was perfect, absolutely perfect. Her attention settled on the horses, and one in particular. 'Will Midnight behave himself?' she asked worriedly. The gelding had a reputation for being naughty.

'Surprisingly, he's taken to it like a duck to water,' Nathan said. He was at the horses' heads, his hand on the reins as he held the animals steady, and she noticed he was wearing coattails and was carrying a top hat under his arm. 'Madam, your carriage awaits.' He bowed deeply and gestured to it.

'We'll meet you there,' Megan said, giving her a kiss. 'Let's get you and your fabulous dress settled, then we'll be off. Your dad can sit one side, and Amos the other. Lena will take Amory and your mum in her car. Is that okay?'

'It's perfect,' Petra said.

She walked carefully towards the carriage, admiring its white woodwork, which had been freshly painted, and the large old-fashioned wheels.

Her dad opened the door for her and shoved a small set of steps in front of it. 'Petra, you look beautiful. I'm so incredibly proud of you,' he said, bringing fresh tears to her eyes. For years she'd thought she was a disappointment to him, having not gone to university and working in Amos's stables instead. To have him say he was proud of her nearly set her off crying again.

'I love you, my darling girl.' Her mum wrapped her arms around her carefully, so as to avoid crushing the dress or smudging her makeup. 'Promise me we'll see more of each other? Now that your dad is taking early retirement, we can visit more often, if that's all right with you?'

'Of course it's all right. I love you too, Mum. And you, Dad.'

Gosh, this wedding was turning out to be far more emotional than Petra had anticipated. She couldn't believe how weepy she felt, nor how her heart was filled with so much love that she thought it might burst.

'I'm getting married,' she said, beaming widely as she climbed into the carriage. In a little over an hour, she'd be Mrs Milton!

She settled herself in the middle of the seat, her bridesmaid's fussing around her, arranging her skirt so it didn't get trodden on, when Petra abruptly stiffened.

She suddenly knew what had been bothering her.

Slowly she raised her head and looked up at the fields above the stables.

Beyond them lay open moorland, where sheep grazed and skylarks nested. At this time of year, it was cloaked in gold and russet from the dried grass and the bracken, with the occasional hardy tree reaching for the sky.

Petra squinted, trying to see past Amos who was heaving himself up the little steps, and she peered around him.

Then she inhaled sharply and her stomach dropped to her boots.

That wasn't smoke from a barbeque that she could smell – it was smoke from a grass fire.

Even as she finally understood what it was, a whisp of grey crept over the horizon...And she knew without a shadow of a doubt that she wouldn't be getting married today.

Because the mountain above the stables was on fire.

Stephen took a cup of tea into the living room and glared at the TV. He wasn't in the mood to watch anything, so he turned the radio on instead. The house tended to be depressingly quiet if he didn't put something on. Besides, if left to his own devices he knew he'd dwell on the last time he'd seen Julie. She kept popping into his head at the most inopportune of moments, and once she was there he had a devil of a job shifting her.

Although he didn't particularly feel like marking the exercise books he'd brought home from school yesterday, it would give him something to do and it might even stop him thinking about his wife for a while, so he sat down at the table and started work.

'Dear lord,' he grumbled, as he opened the first book and noticed the state of it.

The pupil in question had only been given the book three days ago, yet the child had already managed to tear the first page, scribble out most of whatever he'd written on the second, and drawn a cross-section of an eyeball on the fourth (he'd skipped the third page for some reason). The drawing wasn't bad but it had nothing whatsoever to do with glaciation, which was the topic he'd introduced to this particular class last week. The child had only gone and done his Biology homework in his Geography exercise book.

Stephen snorted as he imagined Abbie Cole's expression when she was presented with a paragraph on how U-shaped valleys were formed. The young science teacher would not be amused.

Thinking of Abbie made him feel old. These days teaching was a fast-moving profession, with so many new initiatives and increasing number of boxes to tick and hoops to jump through that he was more than ready to throw in the towel. He'd been planning on doing precisely that when Julie had dropped her bombshell on him.

He'd needed the familiarity and stability of his job during the past academic year, but with his new resolution to go travelling, he'd already started the ball rolling and had announced that he'd be retiring at October half term. He should have been excited about this new chapter in his life, but the only emotion he was feeling at the moment was apprehension – he simply wasn't sure he felt up to travelling alone. He was supposed to have been doing this with his wife by his side, and he was worried that the experience would be empty without someone to share it with.

Stephen sat up straighter and his ears pricked up. Something on the radio had caught his attention, something about a wildfire and Picklewick?

He put his pen down, turned up the volume and listened intently.

"...fire fighters are on the scene and are tackling the blaze. A spokesman told us that the recent dry weather has led to a spate of grass fires across the region, and the stiff easterly breeze today will hinder attempts to extinguish this one. She assures the public that there is no immediate danger to life, but they are keeping a close eye on the situation. At present the blaze is confined to the hillsides to the north and east of the village, and fire fighters are confident they will be able to contain it. We'll keep you updated as events unfold, but there is no need to panic at this moment in time.'

As soon as Stephen heard the word "panic" that was exactly what he felt like doing, until common sense kicked in. The radio said the fire was nowhere near Picklewick and they had every confidence in being able to contain it, so there was no need for him to worry.

But contain it wasn't the same as extinguishing it, was it? And Stephen was aware that grass fires, if they penetrated the surface of the soil, could smoulder for days. Weeks, even.

He turned the radio's volume down and picked up his pen again, ready to do some more marking, but then he paused.

Gazing out of the window, his eyes lost their focus as his attention turned inward.

He thought about Picklewick's location.

Then he thought about it in relation to Muddypuddle Lane and the cottage he and Julie had stayed in.

He might be wrong but...

Stephen reached for his phone, noticing that Isaac had sent him a photo of him and Nelly dressed in their finest. They were off to Petra's wedding today, and that was why he was a little concerned. He wasn't overly worried, but he did have a prickle of unease in the back of his mind, and it was only marginally alleviated when Isaac answered his call.

'Hi, Dad? Did you see the photo? I think we scrub up well. Ow! Nelly just elbowed me. What?' Isaac mumbled something Stephen couldn't hear. 'She said that I scrub up well – **she** always looks this gorgeous.' Isaac laughed, and Stephen heard Nelly's giggle in the background.

He hated to dampen their spirits but...

'The two of you look lovely,' he said, 'but that's not why I called. The radio has just announced that there is a wildfire on the hillside above Picklewick. Have you heard anything?'

'No, not a thing.' Stephen heard the rumble of a car engine and he guessed they were on their way to the church, as Isaac continued, 'Now you mention it though, there is a smoky smell in the air. I assumed someone was burning their garden rubbish. Oh, shit!'

'What?' Stephen's heart sank.

'We are just coming into Picklewick now and there's smoke on the mountain. Nelly, are you thinking what I'm thinking?' Isaac paused, then said, 'It's above the stables on Muddypuddle Lane. Hang on a minute.' Another pause and Stephen heard voices, but he couldn't make out what they were saying. 'Dad? I've got to go. I've just seen Harry and he's heading up to the stables. Petra is worried about the horses, and Harry said that Amos thinks the old guy who owns the farm further up the lane might need a hand to get his sheep off the hillside.'

'Isaac? Isaac! What do you mean **need a hand**? You're not going up there, are you? You don't know the first thing about sheep.'

'It's all hands on deck, Dad. I'll keep you posted. Bye!'

Stephen slowly lowered the phone. The prickling worry had grown into a nagging stab. He knew that Isaac wouldn't be content to stand by and watch. He'd want to do what he could to help.

Pushing the marking to one side, Stephen reached for his phone again. He knew it was pointless to try to call Isaac back, but there was bound to be something about it on social media – there always was.

'At least get changed first,' Petra's mother told her. Everyone had piled into the kitchen and the room was packed.

'There's no time to spare.' Petra had kicked off her delicate sandals and was stuffing her feet into a pair of dirty wellies. She caught Megan's eye and sighed. Turning her back to her maid-of-honour she said, 'Undo me, will you? October, can you go upstairs and fetch me a pair of jodhpurs and a tee shirt?'

'Of course. I'll get changed as well.'

'Me, too.' Charity was already heading for the stairs and Petra sent them a grateful smile, thankful that they'd got ready for the wedding here, rather than in their own houses.

Amos toed off his shiny shoes and Petra glared at him. 'Don't even think it,' she warned. 'I need you to take care of Amory.'

'I can do that,' Lena said.

Petra widened her eyes at the woman, and Lena caught her meaning.

Lena said, 'But maybe it's best if Amos has him. The poor little mite is bound to pick up that something is wrong.' She handed the baby over to Amos, and Petra sent her a small smile of thanks.

The last thing Petra needed right now was Amos overdoing it and having an angina attack. She'd have enough on her plate in getting the horses down from the top field. She could already hear the occasional whinny of distress through the open window as the animals picked up the scent of the growing fire. If she didn't act soon, they might bolt and injure themselves.

'There,' Megan said, indicating that Petra could take the dress off, and Megan hurriedly helped her out of it.

Not in the slightest bit self-conscious as she stood there in her lacy underwear, she shouted up the stairs, 'Hurry up!' and when she heard October coming down them she held her arms out for October to fling her clothes down to her.

Petra knew they didn't have a moment to spare as she dragged the jodhpurs on and yanked the tee shirt over her head. She put the wellies back on and stuffed her phone into her pocket.

Nathan was already leading Storm and Midnight to the lower field where they'd be safe for the time being, having unharnessed them as soon as he'd become aware of the situation.

He'd thrown his top hat onto the seat of the carriage, his suit jacket following, and had started to unbuckle the horses, Luca helping. She knew the two men would catch up with her as soon as they were able.

'Let's go,' she urged, heading for the door.

'What can we do to help?' her dad called after her.

'Make tea, lots of tea. I've got a feeling we're going to need it.'

With October and Charity by her side, Petra raced into the tack room and grabbed an armful of lead ropes.

'Here.' She thrust them at her stable hands, and reached for some more.

If push came to shove, she'd ride one of the horses down and herd the others, but she'd prefer a more orderly descent. It all depended on how far and how fast the fire travelled, and on how successful the fire fighters were at blocking it. The smoke was already thicker, the breeze carrying it down the hillside to sweep across the valley below.

She shot out of the tack room and ran across the yard, skidding to a halt when she heard the sound of engines coming up the lane.

Harry was in the lead with Timothy (she was grateful for the vet's presence but prayed there would be no need for his professional services), but she was surprised to see Isaac and Nelly in the car behind. She gave them a quick smile, before turning her attention back to Harry.

'We're going to bring the horses down now,' she told him. 'Nathan and Luca have just taken Storm and Midnight to the bottom field.'

'I'll park the car and follow you up,' Harry said, and just as she was about to shoot off, he added, 'I love you.'

'I love you, too,' she called over her shoulder, wishing she had time to tell him how handsome he looked in his morning suit.

She was racing up the hill, breathless and anxious when her phone rang.

It was Amos. 'I've just spoken to Harry and he's on his way, but I've asked Timothy to check on Walter. I'm not sure how fast the fire is travelling, and he may have some injured sheep on his hands.'

Damn! Walter! The elderly gent would have trouble rounding the critters up, she knew.

'As soon as the horses are safe, we'll head back up and see what we can do to help with the sheep,' she said.

'Isaac and Nelly are here – as soon as they've got changed, I've suggested they go with Timothy. They can help hold gates open and whatnot.'

'Okay, let me know how they get on.'

'Will do. And Petra? Take care, eh?'

'I will,' she promised.

'Isaac? Isaac? Answer your goddamn phone, son.' Stephen left a message and glared at his mobile. He assumed that as he couldn't get through, Isaac must already be at the stables.

He didn't like to think of him up there, not with a grass fire bearing down. Although there weren't many trees and he didn't think the situation would be as bad as the wildfires in California and Australia that had been on the news in the past, he knew from when he and Julie were up on that very same hillside a couple of weeks ago, that the bracken was head height and tinder-dry. Flames could sweep through it and the dried grass at a rate of knots.

He bit his lip, worry coursing through him. Then he cursed himself for being silly.

It was unlikely that the stables themselves would be in any danger, and he hadn't seen much about it on social media, so it couldn't be that bad, so surely he was fretting over nothing. He doubted that the farm further up Muddypuddle Lane would be at risk, either

But he still couldn't prevent himself from fussing. No matter how old your kids were, you still worry about them, he thought, trying to convince himself that he was overreacting, and he sat down at the table again and eyed the pile of exercise books with dislike. Then sighing heavily, he got to his feet once more and began to pace, and every so often he'd look at his phone as though he expected it to magically burst into life.

Should he try Isaac again?

Stephen shook his head. It would be pointless. When Isaac got a signal he'd call. Until then, he'd simply have to wait.

But that was the problem – he **couldn't** wait.

He was worried, and no amount of telling himself he was being silly would stop him.

Amos! He'd answer, surely?

Hastily Stephen looked up the phone number for the stables and dialled it.

'Hello?' Amos sounded flustered.

'It's Stephen Richards, Isaac's dad. Sorry to bother you, but I wondered if everything was all right? I spoke to Isaac and he said he was on his way to help. Has he arrived yet?'

'He has. He and Nelly have gone up to the farm at the top of the lane to see if the bloke who owns it needs a hand.'

That's what Stephen was worried about. 'He's not answering his phone,' he said.

'I expect he will when he gets to Walter's farm. Parts of the lane can be a dead spot. Sorry, I've got to go, I can hear sirens.'

'Sirens?' Stephen asked, but Amos had already rung off and dread flared in his chest and caught in his throat.

He couldn't stay here and fret – he'd wear a hole in the carpet.

He dialled Julie's number, his heart leaping traitorously when she answered.

'Have you heard from Isaac?' he demanded without any preamble.

'No, why? What's happened?'

'There's a fire on the mountain above the stables,' he said. 'It's on the local radio.'

He heard Julie's exasperated sigh and winced. 'You had me worried for a minute,' she said. 'He's nowhere near the stables. The wedding is taking place in Picklewick. I do hope the stables will be okay though – but I'm sure it will be. These things usually burn themselves out, don't they?'

'Not always. The radio said the fire brigade are at the scene.'

'There you go, then. I don't know what you're worrying about.' She sounded cross.

Stephen sucked in a deep breath. 'I've just spoken to Amos. Isaac isn't in Picklewick; he's gone to the stables to help. And Amos had to ring off because he heard sirens.'

Julie was silent for a second. When she spoke, her voice was strained. 'Pick me up in five minutes.'

Another wave of unease swept over him.

Julie hadn't tried to convince him he was being silly: she was just as anxious as he.

'Timothy?' Harry yelled into his phone. 'Can you hear me?'

He and Petra were heading back up the lane after depositing the last of the ponies in the field. They'd had a bit of a to-do because two fire engines had come racing up the lane as they were coming down it, sirens blaring and blue lights flashing, and the four ponies she and Harry had been leading had spooked. They'd had a devil's own job to calm them down. Nathan was in the field now, checking them over.

Petra swiped a loose strand of hair from her face, and pursed her lips. Harry had been trying to call Timothy on and off for the past fifteen minutes without any luck. Each time Timothy answered, the phone would go dead. Mostly, he failed to answer at all.

'I'm going up there,' Harry said.

'I'll go with you.'

'No.'

Petra blinked. 'You can't tell me what to do,' she objected. If Timothy was in trouble, she didn't intend to sit on her hands and do nothing.

'No,' Harry repeated. 'It's too dangerous.'

'If it's too dangerous for me, it's too dangerous for you,' she reasoned. Fire fighters were tackling the blaze on two fronts, and gusts of smoke-laden air poured down the hill, hot and acrid.

For the first time since she'd realised there was a problem, Petra began to fear for the stables. She was desperate to go up there to see the situation for herself, so she could decide whether all the other residents of the stables needed to be evacuated, human and animal.

At the moment they were safe enough, and Walter's farm was still standing, but seeing the fire engines race past had given her the heebie-jeebies.

'You need to stay with Amory,' Harry said, and fear stabbed her in the stomach as she heard the subtext behind his words – they couldn't risk something awful happening, and for Amory to be without both his parents.

'Don't go,' she said, catching hold of his arm. 'Please.'

'I have to. Timothy is up there.'

'It's not that dangerous, is it? I mean, they would have said. They would have evacuated Walter if it was.'

'It probably isn't,' Harry said. 'But I don't want to take any chances. Watch out!'

Harry yanked her to the side as three ewes careened past and charged off down the lane. 'Nathan!' he yelled, waving his arms.

Nathan was closing the gate, and he looked up when he heard his name being called.

'Sheep!' Harry shouted, cupping his hands around his mouth. He pointed vigorously, and Nathan nodded to show he understood.

Petra saw him open the gate as the sheep came into view, and she watched in relief as he shepherded them into the field. They'd be okay in there for now. If they'd had made it as far as the road, it could have been a disaster.

Harry's phone ringing made her jump, and her heart was in her mouth as he hastened to answer it.

'Timothy!' he cried. 'Are you all right?'

There was a crackle then, 'cut off... Isaac and Nell... shelter... valley... for now... fire...' That was all they heard before the line went dead.

Petra looked at Harry in horror. 'What do you think that meant?'

'That Isaac and Nelly have got cut off? With or without Timothy. God, if anything happens to him, I don't know what I'll do.'

'Go,' Petra urged, against every instinct she had. She wanted to drag him back to the house and force him to stay there until it was safe to go back outside, but she knew he had to find his brother.

'Nathan!' she cried, as her stable manager caught up with them. He was breathing hard and looked tired. 'Harry's going up the mountain,' she told him. 'Timothy tried to phone but the line was dreadful. We think he might have got cut off. Isaac and Nelly, too. Go with him?' She looked at Harry and Nathan followed her gaze. 'Keep him safe?' she pleaded.

Nathan gave her a keen look and nodded once.

Petra let out a breath. He knew what she meant.

Dear god, she prayed as she watched them walk away, please don't let anything happen to them.

'Any news?' Amos pounced on Petra as soon as she stepped through the door.

Julie stared at her, seeing the tightness around the woman's eyes and the tense set of her jaw. Petra was worried, which made Julie worry even more. She and

Stephen had arrived about twenty minutes ago and she'd been on pins ever since.

Petra glanced at her then looked away, holding her hands out for the baby, and when he was safely in her arms she nuzzled the fine hair on the top of his fuzzy head.

That brief look made Julie's blood run cold. 'What is it?' she demanded, catching Stephen's eye and seeing her own fear reflected in their depths. He'd noticed it, too.

Ever since he'd phoned to tell her that their son might be in danger, she'd been scared out of her wits. She knew it was unlikely Isaac would come to any harm, but you heard such dreadful stories and after the things she'd seen on the news, she didn't want him anywhere near a wildfire, no matter how small it might be.

The sirens had set her heart racing until October and Charity had come in to say that the noise had been made by a couple more fire engines going up the hill. Julie had thought it might be an ambulance and dread had caked her heart in ice.

'Where's Luca?' Petra asked.

'He's at the farm, digging up the field above it,' October said.

Petra nodded. 'Good thinking. I didn't know he could drive a tractor?'

'Amos gave him a crash course.'

'Why is he digging up a field?' Julie demanded. What use was that? Luca, whoever he was, should be out there, trying to put this damned thing out.

Amos explained, 'Bare earth will create a firebreak, stop it in its tracks.'

'Walter wanted to use his ploughshare,' October said, 'but it was rusted to hell. I remembered we had one in the barn, so I suggested he used that. Anyway, he looked dreadful, really unwell, so it's better if Luca does it.'

'I'm going back out,' Petra announced, gently placing her son in Megan's arms. 'I can't stay here and—' She broke off and sent Charity the same look she'd given Julie a few moments ago.

'What is it?' Julie felt sick, her skin clammy, her heart pounding. 'What aren't you telling us?'

'Where's Timothy?' Charity was staring at Petra, her eyes wide with fear.

'He's...um...I don't know,' Petra admitted. 'Harry has gone to look for him. Timothy tried to phone, but we couldn't hear him properly. He kept breaking up. I...er...think they might have got cut off.'

A moan rose up in Julie's chest and into her throat. She turned to Amos. 'Didn't you say Isaac and Nelly were with Timothy?' And when he nodded, his eyes brimming with sympathy, the moan escaped her lips.

Suddenly she felt strong arms around her, holding her tight. 'They'll be all right,' Stephen crooned in her ear. 'They'll be all right, I promise.'

'You can't know that.' Julie twisted around to face him. 'Don't make promises you can't keep.'

His gaze was intense as he stared deep into her eyes. 'I never do.'

She looked away, blinking back tears. What a time to bring up the fact that she'd broken a fundamental one of hers.

As if reading her mind, he whispered. 'That's not what I meant.'

'Isn't it?'

Before he had a chance to reply, Petra's phone rang. She was half out of the door, but she stopped and took it out of her pocket.

The kitchen was totally silent as she said, 'Harry?'

Julie saw Petra's shoulders sag, and she bit back a sob.

'Thank the lord!' Petra cried. 'Where were they...? And you're sure they're all right? How about everyone else?' She stepped back into the room, her face wreathed in smiles, and gave them a thumbs up.

Julie slumped against Stephen, feeling weak with relief, and his arms tightened around her as he held her up. She was shaking and tears poured down her face.

Petra's eyes widened and her mouth dropped open. 'Are you serious? If you think we can... Oh, you have, have you?... I can't wait—' Abruptly Petra stopped talking and a blush spread across her face. 'I...erm...have an audience,' she said. 'I'll be ready... Of course they can – the more the merrier. But are they sure the fire is out?'

Julie was hanging on Petra's every word, and so were the others. Even the baby was staring intently at his mum, his little chin wet with dribble.

Petra pulled a face and dropped the phone in her pocket. 'That was Harry,' she told them.

'We gathered that.' Amos raised his bushy eyebrows. 'What's the news?'

'The news is that Timothy, Isaac and Nelly are fine. They got caught in the small valley not far from the old farmhouse, so they sheltered in there until the fire passed by. Harry said they got a bit hot and Isaac singed his eyebrows, but they're okay. It was starting to burn itself out at that point, because one of the appliances had saturated the vegetation. They're on the way back. Oh, and you'd all better get changed and clean yourselves up – I'm getting married in an hour!'

CHAPTER NINE

'Doesn't she look beautiful?' Julie whispered in Stephen's ear, her eyes on Petra as Amos helped her climb into the carriage.

'She certainly does,' Stephen agreed, although he secretly thought that Julie had actually been more beautiful on their wedding day, but maybe he was biased.

'I can't believe they've managed to pull it all together in an hour,' she said. 'Even with everyone pitching in, it took some doing.'

It certainly had. Stephen had watched in amazement as Petra had been whisked off upstairs by her bridesmaids. Amos had got on the phone to some chap called William and had arranged for the food for the reception to be sorted out. Nathan, the bloke who managed the stables, had grabbed hold of a guy called Luca as soon as the poor fella had stepped inside the door, and had marched him back out again, saying something about getting the horses hitched up to a carriage. And when Harry and Timothy arrived, it had only been to collect the car and dash off to Timothy's house to get cleaned up. Petra's parents had gone with them because according to Petra's mother, it was going to take a miracle to sort Harry's suit trousers out.

To be fair, most of the flurry of activity had gone over his and Julie's heads, because they only had eyes for their son and his girlfriend, and Julie had smothered Isaac in so many kisses that he'd joked he wouldn't need a wash to get rid of the soot and dirt.

'You look a right state,' Julie had said to Isaac when she'd calmed down a bit. Nelly didn't look much better, but at least the pair of them had been wearing borrowed clothes and not their wedding outfits. 'What happened exactly, and why were you anywhere near the fire in the first place?'

'Can we talk about it later?' Isaac suggested. 'We've got to get to the church.' He'd looked at his borrowed clothes and grimaced.

Julie had wrinkled her nose. 'You need a shower – you smell like a bonfire in an allotment.'

Amos said to Isaac, 'Why don't you and Nelly go and get cleaned up in the cottage next to the one Julie and Stephen stayed in? In fact, why don't you go with them?' he said to Julie. 'Come to the wedding – the more the merrier. I think half the fire department will be there too, although I suspect they'll be more interested in the food afterwards rather than the ceremony.'

So that's what they did. Julie confessed she felt a little self-conscious because she wasn't wearing a dress, but Stephen assured her it didn't matter. He wasn't exactly dressed for the occasion either, with his faded jeans, old chambray shirt and scruffy trainers. But he didn't care. Isaac and Nelly were unhurt, no one had been injured (apart from a daft sheep who had tried to leap a fence and had got tangled up in some wire), the stables and the farm at the end of the lane were also safe, and the wedding was going ahead, although rather later than planned.

Did it matter what they wore?

'I suppose not,' Julie said after he'd said the same thing to her, 'not when you put it like that.'

'Come on, we'd better get going if we don't want to run the risk of arriving at the church **after** the bride,' he said, as the bridesmaids all piled into Luca's Range Rover.

'What a day!' she exclaimed as they hurried towards Stephen's car. 'I certainly never expected all this drama when I got up this morning. I've never been so scared in all my life.'

'Me, neither.' The thought of losing Isaac had been more than he could bear. The fear had been indescribable. He wanted to hug his son to him and never let him out of his sight again.

It came as no surprise to realise that he felt the same way about Julie.

He loved her – he always had done – and the weekend they'd spent at Petra's cottage had made him realise how utterly bereft he felt without her.

So why was he being so stubborn about things?

Julie had hurt him deeply, but he was no longer convinced that she was still pining over her lost love. She'd seemed so happy the morning after the fete, until he'd told her that making love to her had been a mistake. He'd seen how broken she was, and he'd turned his back on her.

Had he been a fool?

The thought that he might have had crept over him when he'd been standing in Amos's kitchen, his arms around her, as they waited to hear whether their son was safe. And he'd had a sudden vision of how he'd feel if he lost Julie too. What if something were to happen to her? What if she became ill? He was finding it hard enough to plod through each day as it was – he'd fall apart if Julie died.

It was a macabre way to view things, but neither of them was getting any younger and every day brought news about people their age passing away. Life was so damned short and could be very cruel, and it had taken Isaac being in danger to make him see that.

Stephen knew he could never forget the hurt Julie had caused, but he could – and did – forgive her. They had been so young and it had happened such a long time ago. Was he prepared to let the past sour his future?

He had to tell her how he felt, and maybe they could start over – this time without any secrets between them.

But now wasn't the time. It could wait until later. Right now they had a wedding to go to.

Petra swallowed nervously. This was really happening – she was getting married! After the events of earlier, she didn't imagine the wedding could possibly go ahead, but Harry – wonderful, handsome, thoughtful Harry – had asked the vicar to put the ceremony on hold, vowing it would take place today. He'd had such faith that everything would be okay, it had made her heart melt.

So here she was, standing outside the church, with her maid-of-honour handing her a bouquet of pale pink and white roses, and grinning madly at her. Amos took his place on her right, her dad on her left, and the bridesmaids behind, in the traditional manner.

Everyone else was already inside, including Nathan, who had handed the horses over to one of the vets who owned the practice where Timothy worked. Petra couldn't imagine getting married without stalwart, dependable Nathan being there to witness it.

The organ which had been playing holding music in the background, struck up the Wedding March, and Petra lifted her chin. She no longer cared whether all eyes were on her. She no longer minded being the centre of attention. All that mattered was that she was marrying the most wonderful man in the world, and she knew everyone was happy for her. Picklewick had come together to make sure her beloved stables was safe, and she was consumed with gratitude for the generosity and selflessness of the villagers.

'Ready?' Amos asked. He was beaming with pride, and she kissed him on the cheek. She gave her dad a kiss too, not wanting him to feel left out. She mightn't have had the best relationship with her parents in the past, but this was a new beginning, and she knew they were happy for her.

'Ready,' she said, and slowly and surely she walked into the church and into her future.

'I know this is a stables and that we're in the middle of an arena,' Julie said, 'but I didn't expect horses to be here.' When Lena had said that Petra lived and breathed horses, she hadn't been wrong.

The horse-drawn carriage that had driven the bride to the church and had brought her and Harry back to the stables had been a lovely touch. But Julie wasn't so sure about seeing a whole herd of the beasts being ridden around the arena by a load of children.

Petra though, was clearly thrilled.

The tables for the wedding guests had been laid out at one end of the large space, and Julie had assumed the other end was meant for dancing – although how anyone would be able to strut their stuff on a floor made of bits of rubber was beyond her.

But no...the area had been kept free for a parade of horses, all decked out with flowers in their bridles. They seemed to be doing some kind of a strange co-ordinated dance, to music no less!

'It's called dressage,' Lena said, seeing her confusion. 'October has been getting them to practice for weeks. It hasn't been easy, because she was only able to do it if Petra was out on a hack. A ride in the hills,' she explained, as Julie's confusion deepened.

'Aw, look, it's the donkey!' Julie cried. Gerald had a panier on his back and was being led to each table for the guests to take a favour out of the basket. 'You liked the donkey, didn't you, Stephen?' She remembered how Stephen had scratched the animal's ears. They'd just returned from a walk, on their first day in the cottage. Such a lot had happened since then – but nothing had actually changed.

She and Stephen were still estranged.

Julie felt a tear or two in her eye and she fanned a hand in front of her face, willing herself not to cry.

'Are you okay?' Stephen asked. He'd been remarkably attentive throughout the course of the ceremony and the reception, and she didn't know what she was supposed to feel or how she was supposed to react. Looking at them, anyone could be forgiven for thinking he doted on her, when the opposite was true.

'I'm fine,' she replied, adding, 'what is it about weddings that make people so emotional?' She didn't want him to think she was upset because of him.

'Perhaps it's because they remember their own, or they wish they were getting married to the love of their lives,' he said.

Julie knew what he was referring to, and even though she knew it wouldn't make the slightest bit of difference, she wanted to put the record straight once and for all.

The horses had been led away, and different music started up. It was a song she vaguely recognised, "Wild Horses" by Natasha Bedingfield, and she saw Harry hold out his hand to his bride. Petra had taken her shoes off and her feet were bare. She looked delirious with happiness and another lump came to Julie's throat.

'Emrys isn't the love of my life,' she said. 'You are.'

Stephen was staring at her with such intensity it scared her.

But when he didn't reply, her heart shattered all over again. He could at least acknowledge her.

Tears blurring her vision, she scrambled to her feet. Other people were rising to theirs as they took to the dance floor, and she dodged around them, desperate to escape. She had to get out of here, she had to get away from Stephen.

Before she had taken more than a few steps, a strong arm caught her around the waist and spun her on her heel. 'Let go,' she began, thinking it was Isaac.

It wasn't.

Stephen had hold of her, and there was such a look of love on his face that it stole her breath.

He said, 'You are the love of my life, too. I don't want to live another day without you in it. I love you, Julie, and I realise that you love me, that you always have.'

She opened her mouth to tell him how much she loved him but she didn't get to say the words, as his lips claimed hers and he kissed her with everything he had.

When he finally pulled away, his eyes dark pools of love and longing, and said, 'Let's get out of here. We've got a whole world to explore – together,' Julie felt the flames of hope reignite in her heart, and she knew she'd follow this man to the ends of the earth and back.

She'd finally laid her ghosts to rest, and she couldn't wait to spend the rest of her life with the man she'd married all those years ago.

The Stables on Muddypuddle Lane Series

Spring

Summer

Autumn

Winter

Valentine Kisses

The Patter of Tiny Feet

Wedding Bells

Christmas

About Etti

Etti Summers is the author of wonderfully romantic fiction with happy ever afters guaranteed.

She is also a wife, a mum, a pink gin enthusiast, a veggie grower and a keen reader.